Dear So-Called Reader:

If you are reading this right now, it might be because you are somebody who enjoyed our TV show. Or maybe it's because you've heard about the show and you're curious. Or maybe you're just bored and don't have anything else to do. Whatever your reason for picking up this book, I'm glad you did. These are characters who have been a part of my life for a few years now. I've come to love them all. I hope you do too.

—Winnie Holzman

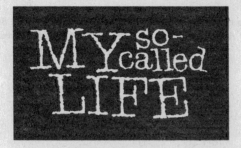

MY so-called LIFE

by Catherine Clark

*A novel based on the television series
created by Winnie Holzman*

Random House Sprinters™
Random House 🏠 New York

*Special thanks to Nancy Allen of Marquee Images, and to
Michael Ross and Randi Cohen of abc Productions.
Thanks also to USA Weekend magazine and to Sassy magazine.*

*Additional thanks to Wendy Hashmall, Kate Klimo, Lisa Banim,
Alice Alfonsi, Georgia Morrissey, Gretchen Schuler, and
Jacqueline Dwyer of Random House.*

Photo credits:
Jenny Gummersall: p. 216; Danny Feld: p. 212, 214, 215, 217

ACKNOWLEDGMENTS

Thanks to all the viewers of all ages who wrote me such encouraging and heartfelt letters. Thanks to the writers who contributed scripts: Adam Dooley, Elisabeth Gill, Liberty Godshall, Jill Gordon, Ellen Herman, Richard Kramer, Justin Tanner, and Betsy Thomas. A very special thanks to Jason Katims, for his brilliant writing, his positive energy, and his over-all coolness. Thanks to our amazing cast: Bess Armstrong, Wilson Cruz, Claire Danes, Devon Gummersall, Tom Irwin, A. J. Langer, Jared Leto, Devon Odessa, and Lisa Wilhoit. Thanks to Ted Harbert at ABC for letting us tell our stories our way. A huge thank-you to Alan Poul. Thanks also to Monica Wyatt, Diane Driscoll, Jenifer Catalano, Art Rusis, Mark Saltzman, Natalie Robbins, and the entire crew of *My So-Called Life*.

My gratitude to Marshall Herskovitz and Ed Zwick—for more reasons than I can say. Thanks to Scott Winant, for being the director I always dreamed of. Finally, thanks to my husband, Paul Dooley, and my daughter, Savannah—for everything.

—Winnie Holzman

FOREWORD

"*My So-Called Life* is about normal kids who are self-conscious and imperfect. Before this show came on, I didn't realize how normal I am."

—Laura Buck, 16, Illinois

"In this trying time to come of age, it is so nice to see wonderful television that is so similar to my own life. This is a rare show that raises questions and stirs up conversations in our household."

—Carrie Bennett, 15, Colorado

"All the other shows about teenagers are really fake or insult our lifestyle and our intelligence. I hope to see *My So-Called Life* on the air again."

—Katy Mlynarski, 14, Connecticut

"It's the first show in a really long time that I can honestly relate to. And it's not just teens who enjoy the show; my parents watch it with me. I think the things that go on in Angela's life and how she reacts to them show my parents what is going on in my head sometimes."

—Tara Goshorn, 15, Pennsylvania

There have been many popular television series over the years, but few have created the kind of passion and loyalty found among the fans of *My So-Called Life*.

From the start, the critics raved about this well-written program. They called it better than first-rate and even described its lead character, fifteen-year-old Angela Chase, as a '90s female version of Holden Caulfield, the troubled teenager of J. D. Salinger's *The Catcher in the Rye*.

The comparison to a literary classic seems fitting, because classic literature plays an important role in the show—from *Anne Frank: The Diary of a Young Girl* and Franz Kafka's "Metamorphosis" to a Shakespearean sonnet and a Thornton Wilder play. In the series, literature becomes a way for the characters to better understand and appreciate life and each other, to connect and make connections. So it seems right that the series itself has undergone a metamorphosis and taken on literary form.

The novel you are now holding is based on the first season's episodes of *My So-Called Life*, which were originally aired in late 1994 and early 1995. Although it was impossible for Catherine Clark to include every scene from the drama, she wonderfully captures the spirit of the show, and many of its memorable moments. We hope that the book, like the television show, will make you think and make you feel.

Alice Alfonsi
Editor, Random House

Chapter 1

Angela Chase was looking at the world from underneath her acrylic turtleneck sweater. She felt like she was underwater, looking up at things through pink, filtered sunlight and tangled weeds. *The way it probably feels when you're drowning.*

"What should the theme be?" Ms. Mayhew, the yearbook adviser, asked.

The theme, thought Angela. As if you could take an entire school of people and give them a theme. What a ridiculous idea. Almost as ridiculous as her liking Jordan Catalano, who was not even aware of things like yearbooks and themes.

Or her.

But Jordan was all she was aware of at the moment. His brown hair. His shoulders. His slouch. That rawhide necklace he wore that would have looked stupid on anyone else. His brown jacket with that fake sheepskin collar, like something somebody on an old, bad Western TV series would have worn. But it wasn't just his looks. It was his *eyes*. Those lighter-and-clearer-than-you-expected-them-to-be blue eyes. *Isn't that a Crayola color?*

Sometimes she tried to send Jordan psychic messages, an Angela bolt or something. *Think about me as much as I'm thinking about you. Please?* But she knew. *Psychic bolts don't ask or say please. They just...well, bolt.*

"It's like...he has this way of leaning," Angela had told her friend Rayanne Graff that morning. Not that Angela could even find words to describe the things about Jordan that made him the way he was—infinitely attractive.

Angela had started hanging out with Rayanne a few weeks ago, at the beginning of September. She couldn't even remember exactly how it had happened. Just one day in the girls' bathroom, where it seemed like she spent more time than in any of her classes. And why not, she thought. She actually learned more in there than she did in science. How to put on eyeliner (from Rickie Vasquez, Rayanne's other best friend, who hung out in the girls' room even though he wasn't supposed to). Where to go on Friday nights (the Pike Street Bar & Grill). Why there was never any soap in the dispenser (school staff cutbacks). That there was fat in gravy (okay, so that was pretty obvious). How to French-braid her hair, which was now, incidentally, bright, flaming red instead of its old boring, dirty-blond former self.

She, Rayanne, and Rickie had colored it at her house the day before. "Say 'colored,' not 'dyed,'" Rayanne had instructed her. "Because nobody wants to walk around with *dead* hair."

"On the other hand? I hate it when people call me

colored," Rickie added. "It's, like, so offensive when older people call me that."

"They do? Still?" Angela had asked him, horrified. Although she could imagine her grandfather saying something dumb like that, and not understanding that it was rude.

"What happened?!" Angela's mother had shrieked when she saw Angela, as if she really *had* died. Or her hair. Or whatever. Her mother had obviously thought something was very, very wrong. Like there was a major tragedy. Patty Chase took everything a little too seriously, or the wrong things seriously, and the important things she didn't even notice. Angela couldn't even stand to eat a well-balanced meal at home lately, because it made her mother *so* happy. As if Angela's eating habits had anything to do with...anything.

Anyway, one day there was Sharon Cherski being her best friend, and the next there was Rayanne. Angela couldn't even explain it, exactly. It just seemed like if she didn't start hanging out with Rayanne, she would die. Death being a *theme*, lately.

Things about Sharon were just getting to me. How people are. How they always expect you to be a certain way. Even your best friend.

Like no one is ever allowed to change, not even their hair color. Maybe the theme for the yearbook should be stagnation, Angela thought. *Utter and complete stagnation. Like...a stinking, mossy swamp. Called Liberty High School.*

Liberty. Right. Tons of freedom everywhere.

So when Rayanne told Angela her hair was holding her back, Angela knew she was right. And it was exciting, because normally someone like Rayanne wouldn't even notice her, much less give her advice. Not to make too much of it, Angela thought, but it was kind of, like...a breakthrough.

Angela peeked through her knit sweater at Sharon, who was sitting next to her. Sharon hadn't quite adjusted to the fact that she was becoming a bit top-heavy, and she always leaned way over in her chair—as if the school desks weren't uncomfortable enough. Sharon was supposedly dating a senior jock named Kyle Vinovich...or so Angela had *heard*. Sharon didn't actually confide in her anymore, or vice versa. Things between them had gotten kind of mucked up.

Ms. Mayhew was now pacing around the front of the room, throwing out themes like they were disposable razors. "Graduation: The Final Frontier. The Apple: Fruit of Knowledge. The Year Two Thousand. Okay, people, let's vote. Who wants the Final Frontier?"

I do, thought Angela. *Right about now*. She watched as a boy to her left tapped the girl in front of him on the head with a straw. Another boy was trying to balance a pencil on the bridge of his nose. *How about this theme: Boys and Sticklike Objects*, Angela thought. *Eyeglasses by Armani, Yearbook by Freud*. In the corner, Brian Krakow, the official yearbook photographer, was adjusting the light meter for his camera.

"All right...we have fifteen people signed up here, and only fourteen votes. Who didn't vote?" Ms. Mayhew asked.

Angela slowly surfaced, pulling the turtleneck down around her neck and pressing her slightly static hair against her face. "Me." She picked up her backpack, stuffed her notebook into it, and stood up. "I don't—"

"Where are you going?" Sharon was staring at her.

"I guess I don't want to be on yearbook," Angela said. "Sorry." She turned and started walking toward the door.

"Well, would you mind telling us why not?" Ms. Mayhew asked.

"No." Angela paused, her hand on the door. "I mean, yes." She glanced over her shoulder at Brian Krakow, who was pointing his camera directly at her face. "I mean, I don't know why." *Maybe because in yearbooks there are no such things as "candids." Nobody wants to show people or see people as they really are. In my humble opinion, the whole point of a school yearbook is to be as* uncandid *as possible. So what's the point of doing it?*

Angela blinked. Rayanne was peering into her eyes with the concentration of an ophthalmologist. "Lipstick. You definitely need some new lipstick to match your new hair."

Angela shrugged. "Whatever."

Rickie was standing in front of the mirror in the girls' bathroom, poking through Rayanne's giant makeup kit. He selected a color and tossed Rayanne the lipstick tube.

"So Rickie," Rayanne said as she leaned closer toward Angela and applied a matte shade called Autumn Sunset. "Angela's in love with Jordan Catalano. We have to help her."

"Ray*anne*!" Angela cried.

Rickie looked over at Angela and smiled.

"Come on, I can tell Rickie." Rayanne stepped back, smearing the lipstick slightly with her pinkie. "I know— come to Tino's party tonight. He'll be there."

"He doesn't even know me." Angela sighed. "If I go, I'll be, like, making a fool of myself. Totally."

Rickie bent toward the mirror, dabbing at a smudge

of liquid eyeliner on his eyelid. "Don't you love how he leans?" He and Angela sighed in unison.

"See, *I* don't get obsessed with guys, so I don't have these problems," Rayanne said confidently, looking at them like they were both crazy.

The bell rang, and Angela jumped. "That's the second bell!" She grabbed her backpack and bolted for the exit.

Then she stopped. Nobody was following her. Rayanne and Rickie hadn't moved one inch. It was as if the bell didn't even apply to their lives. Like they hadn't even heard it; like it was one of those special whistles only nerds could hear.

"I mean...I may as well go to bio," Angela said lamely as she edged out the scarred wooden door. "Since I'm not that busy or anything."

Rayanne looked at her and shrugged. Rickie just kept working on his eyeliner.

Angela wanted to be as cool as both of them, but she just couldn't make herself skip class. So she went out the door—and started running as fast as she could down the deserted hall.

There's something about an empty school hallway, and everyone sitting in their assigned seat in their assigned classroom at the assigned time. It's like...the military or something. Only you don't get the uniform...or maybe you do.

Turning the corner, Angela glanced at a cheerleader who was crouched beside her locker, crying. She felt a pang of sympathy. She kept running.

"Is *Anne Frank: The Diary of a Young Girl* written in the third person? Or the first person?"

Angela was staring at the ceiling, where a flickering

fluorescent bulb was on its way to burning out. Ms. Mayhew was pacing around the classroom, looking for an answer to her question.

"Does she say, '*She* was forced to go into hiding'?" Ms. Mayhew paused.

Angela saw Brian Krakow's hand go up. As always.

"Somebody *besides* Brian," Ms. Mayhew prompted.

Nobody moved.

Ms. Mayhew sighed. "Brian?"

"No," Brian said. "She says, '*I.*'"

"That's right! She says, '*I—I* was forced to go into hiding.' This is called the first person. Okay? This will be on the quiz. And how would you describe Anne Frank?"

"Lucky," whispered Angela. She hadn't even meant to utter the word out loud; it was just a passing thought. But all of a sudden everyone in her class was staring at her intensely. Even Sharon, who looked like she'd just found out that Angela was an alien. A very strange alien. Perhaps from another universe.

Ms. Mayhew frowned at Angela. "Is that supposed to be funny?"

Angela glanced over at Sharon for help, but Sharon was staring uncomfortably at her desk.

"How could you even say something like that?" Ms. Mayhew asked, visibly appalled.

Angela was about to speak, to muster a lame apology, although she didn't even know why she'd said what she did, except that it was in her mind and she obviously believed it to some degree. Then Jordan Catalano walked through the doorway. Like, to her rescue, almost.

But Ms. Mayhew was still staring at Angela and waiting for an explanation. And she had to talk. In front of him. Which was impossible.

She glanced over at Jordan. He was casually tapping a bottle of breath freshener held over his mouth. *He cares whether his breath is fresh or not.* Health and beauty products told a lot about a person. For instance, Brian Krakow had probably never even heard of breath freshener yet. Not that he *needed* it, but he just wasn't, like, conscious of these things.

"Anne Frank perished in a concentration camp! How could Anne Frank be *lucky*?" Ms. Mayhew demanded.

"I don't know," Angela said, blushing as she glanced from Jordan to Sharon to Brian to Jordan to some guy whose name she kept forgetting and back to Ms. Mayhew. "Because she was trapped in an attic for three years with this guy she really liked?" She shrugged.

Sharon just stared at her, both eyebrows raised.

Angela wanted to disappear. *Why do I say these things? Why do I even open my mouth, like, at all?*

Ms. Mayhew lifted a limp tuna-fish sandwich on white bread out of a square green plastic container.

Seeing a teacher's actual lunch is, like, so depressing. Not to mention her bra strap. If Angela, who had only been wearing bras a few years now, could figure out how to keep her straps from slipping, why couldn't someone who was twice her age? You could make them shorter; you could make them longer. Those were the basics covered by the lingerie lady at the department store.

"So, you quit yearbook," Ms. Mayhew said, pushing up her bra strap. "And your hair is red now. I'm really concerned about you, Angela. What's going on?" The bra strap slowly slipped down her shoulder again.

Angela looked away, fidgeting with the strap on her backpack. "I don't know. It just seems like you agree to have a certain personality or something, for no reason, or maybe just to make things easier for other people. But when you think about it, maybe that's not you."

Ms. Mayhew chewed her sandwich. A piece of celery dropped onto the desk. "And how does this apply to dropping off the yearbook staff?"

"I guess...Well, it's like everyone's in this huge hurry to make this book and photograph everyone and write stuff down so we can all remember what happened. But it's not even what really happened—it's what everyone thinks was supposed to happen," Angela continued. "Because if you made a book that was true..."

Angela pictured herself sitting in class half an hour ago, making an inane comment about Anne Frank just as Jordan Catalano walked into the room. She thought of not being friends with Sharon anymore; of Rickie being taunted by bullies because he was bisexual or gay or just because he was *different* from them; of Rayanne drinking too much and not having her father around because he walked out on her. And how every day, just walking down the hall in front of certain guys was like facing a firing squad.

"If you made a book about what really happens, it would be a really upsetting book."

Ms. Mayhew dabbed at a piece of tuna on her lip as she nodded at Angela's comment.

"Anyway, you want some gum?" Angela offered her pack to the teacher and smiled faintly. *It's, like, essential after tuna*, she felt like adding, but restrained herself. Ms. Mayhew still seemed pretty upset with her. In fact, she hadn't stopped frowning at her yet.

Angela looked at her. "Well, I should go. If we're done, I mean."

"So you're not doing yearbook, is that what you said?" Ms. Mayhew asked. "Is that final?"

"I guess," Angela said. Why did Ms. Mayhew care whether she stayed on yearbook or not? Sharon and Brian would probably end up doing the whole thing themselves anyway. It was, like, one of their dreams, probably, now that they were sophomores. To be in *charge* of everything. To control their destiny.

The way Anne Frank hadn't been able to.

The way Angela felt was completely impossible.

At one time, she had believed that there were rules, and that if you followed the rules, things would work out a certain way. If you did your homework, you'd be one kind of person. If you participated in class, you'd be smart. Good things were supposed to come to those who waited—so her mother always told her—good things like boyfriends, perfect bodies, awards, scholarships.

But Angela didn't believe any of those things anymore. So why make a book based on a bunch of falsehoods? How could you look back at a picture of the Chess Club and say *that* was Brian Krakow? Maybe it was him…and maybe it wasn't. Maybe the real him was supposed to be in the Drama Club.

Of course, using Brian as an example was totally ridiculous. If anyone had an identity that hadn't changed in fifteen years, Brian did. Once a brain, always a brain. Angela's neighbor from here to eternity. Or at least until she went away to college.

She couldn't wait.

"Ms. Mayhew?" Angela turned in the doorway. "Do they make yearbooks in college?"

That night, Angela pushed her hair back around her ears

and let out a nervous sigh. So this was it. A party. An actual party. At Tino's house.

She'd never even met Tino, but she knew *of* him. She knew that he had the best parties. And that if she wanted to start living her life instead of just lying on her bed at home thinking about it, she had to just plunge right through the crowd, find Jordan, and start talking to him.

Yeah. Right.

She peered over the dozens of people surrounding her, dancing to loud music in the fenced yard. Actually, mostly the boys were dancing; the girls were standing around in small clumps, yelling their normally whispered comments. On a stage under a harsh light at the back of the yard, a band was plowing its way through a song.

Angela was briefly happy that Tino didn't live in her neighborhood. Her mother was the kind of person who would walk over and tell the band to turn the volume down. Then she'd stand there arguing with Tino about what was "decent" and "considerate" and "right." *Totally humiliating.* Or else she'd probably just call the cops.

For Angela, just getting out of the house that night had been a major battle. She hated lying. She wasn't good at it. And telling her father that she was at an extra-credit play rehearsal for school was a really dumb idea. When was she supposed to actually perform in this play?

Angela stared out at the crowd in the yard, searching desperately for Rayanne. All she could see was that everyone was wearing lots of black, and lots of flannel shirts and jeans. She, on the other hand, was definitely overdressed in a short-sleeved dress with tiny flowers on it. But right now, that was the least of her problems. She needed to find Rayanne.

Suddenly, she caught a glimpse of her girlfriend's hair. She was dancing with a senior Angela vaguely recognized. "Rayanne!" she called. "Rayanne!"

Rayanne took a swig out of a silver flask and turned in her direction. She didn't seem to see Angela.

Angela pushed through the crowd toward her. "Rayanne!"

Rayanne started waving wildly at her, and Angela began to smile with some amount of relief. Maybe tonight would be fun after all—*fun* being a relative concept. Angela tried to edge her way around a group of wildly dancing boys. The yard had turned into a big mud pit, and her combat boots made a slurping, sucking sound with each step.

All of a sudden, a boy jumped up onstage, jumped off, and came flying through the air toward her. Struggling to dodge him, Angela slipped and crashed onto the sloppy ground, stomach first.

Lying there, sprawled on her face, Angela felt like she was in a U.S. Army ad—the one that convinced you never to join the armed forces, ever, because moments like this would be happening to you constantly.

Slowly getting up, she peeled her wet, muddy dress away from her skin. It made a disgusting sucking sound like a clingy bathing suit. A few kids to the left of her were staring at her, mouths agape, as if she'd just crept out of the black lagoon. She turned and went toward Tino's house. Maybe she could clean up in the bathroom. Or maybe Tino would lend her some clothes. Just exactly what size person *was* Tino, anyway? Or, better yet, maybe she could hide in his house until everyone else went home.

She came up to the back door, turned the knob, and

walked into the dark house. She closed the door behind her, leaning on it and releasing a heavy sigh. That's when she noticed the body. It was slouched in a recliner in front of the TV, slouched down so low, and so motionless, the person seemed to be asleep—or dead.

Then the body moved. It was Jordan Catalano.

Chapter 2

Jordan briefly glanced over at Angela, then looked back at the television. He was watching a music video, but he had pressed the mute button. Women in bustiers and miniskirts danced silently on the screen, their bodies flashing across Jordan's face, flickering shadows in the dark room.

Angela took a few steps closer to him and peered at the screen, pretending she was interested. She perched on the arm of the couch and waited. For somebody to say something. And for it to be the right thing. Or anything at all.

Jordan yawned and shifted slightly in the recliner. "This doesn't seem like a Friday," he finally said.

Angela awkwardly pulled at the torn shoulder of her dress. "It's...Thursday," she told him, her voice almost shaking. *How can one person have so much power over you? How?*

"Oh." Jordan looked confused. "Are you sure?"

"Well, yesterday was Wednesday, so…"

"Oh. Right."

"So that's how I know." *I'm a logic genius, actually. God, could I sound any dumber? Why can't I say something interesting or witty or—*

Three boys opened the door. They didn't come in. "Catalano, this bites," the tall one said. "Let's go to Pike Street."

Jordan stood up almost automatically, pushing his hands against the arms of the recliner and then striding past Angela as if she weren't even there. The door closed behind him with a resounding bang.

Angela put her face in her hands and sank down onto the couch. *Is it, like, humanly possible for things to actually get worse than this?*

*In my humble opinion…*She touched the muddy, torn fabric of her dress. *No.*

"You should have seen my mother last night when I got home," Angela told Rickie and Rayanne in the lunch line the next day. "She went, like, ballistic when I showed up in this muddy, ripped dress. I mean, she must have thought I got run over or something."

"Or something," Rickie said, putting a dish of yellowish pudding on his tray. "At least your parents care."

"Oh, yeah. It's great," Angela said.

"Well, I had an okay time." Rayanne poked at a dish of lime Jell-O and watched it wobble. "But tonight? There's this rave, at that club—Let's Bolt. I know Tino can get us in. And I guarantee, Jordan Catalano will be there."

"Rayanne, I *told* you. We have nothing to say to each other. It's, like…completely embarrassing." *That's putting it mildly*, Angela thought. *More like life-crushing.*

"But it's perfect!" Rayanne protested. "You won't have to think of anything to say to him, because nobody can even *hear* anybody at Let's Bolt."

"I don't know," Angela said slowly as they walked out into the cafeteria, carrying their trays. Angela winced as a group of jocks shoved Brian Krakow's tray up toward him, flattening a large piece of lasagna onto his shirt.

The cafeteria is the embarrassment capital of the world. Every day, it's like a prison movie. Only there's no redemption.

"I don't have anything to wear to a place like Let's Bolt, anyway," Angela told Rayanne.

"So I'll lend you something," Rayanne said, shrugging. "You have to look tough, you know. Somebody once set fire to my hair at Let's Bolt."

"*Excuse* me? Why?" Angela asked, automatically reaching up to touch her own head.

"So...should we sit somewhere?" Rickie looked around the cafeteria.

"Because they hated it," Rayanne explained. "It's okay, though, Tino put it out."

Angela stared at Rayanne's hair, trying to find the singed part.

"There's nowhere to sit," Rickie complained.

Where you sit in the cafeteria is way too important. You feel like it's going to have this effect on your whole future. Everyone has their own section—the jocks, the druggies, the nerds, the Models Inc. group. And if you don't have a section? You're, like...nobody.

That was why it was good to be friends with Rayanne. Every section was her section. Angela slid into a seat across from Rayanne and glanced around the cafeteria, looking for Jordan. As far as she could tell, Jordan didn't eat, at least not in any organized kind of way. He didn't go to his classes, he didn't eat lunch, he didn't play on any teams, and he definitely didn't "participate in extracurricular activities," the way Angela's guidance counselor was always urging her to. So what did he do all day? And why did he bother coming to school anyway? It *couldn't* be the social life.

No, it really couldn't be, Angela thought, as a group of cheerleaders sitting at the table behind her erupted into a spontaneous shriek.

Can't people just cheer on their own? Like...to themselves?

"I'd have to think of a really good lie," Angela told Rayanne in the girls' bathroom after lunch. For once, Rickie wasn't with them. "That thing about the extra credit and the play and everything? That won't work again. I mean, it barely even worked the first time."

Rayanne fiddled with the long piece of curled blond hair she wore in front of her face. "Simple. Say that you're spending the night at my place."

The door creaked open and swung drastically shut with a bang. Sharon Cherski walked in, stared at Angela and Rayanne for a second, then kept going, to the sink by the window. She pulled out a long string of dental floss.

That's Sharon. I mean, how responsible can a person get? To, like, floss after every single meal. Sometimes Sharon seems like a warped version of my mother...only with larger breasts.

Sharon had shoulder-length brown hair, which she was constantly adjusting into different hair accessories, and she wore lots of dresses and skirts. "Nice things," as Angela's mother described them.

It was weird, but when Sharon and Rayanne were in the same room, Angela had no idea which one to talk to.

"And it's the perfect lie," Rayanne went on, after an irritated glance at Sharon. "Because you can stay over, after. My mom won't even be there. Anyway, I have to take off and find Tino. Just think about how great it would be." She stuffed her makeup kit back into her shoulder bag and flounced out of the bathroom, leaving Angela standing there, and Sharon...flossing.

Angela turned on the faucet and held her hands under the freezing cold water, just to have something to do. Sharon dangled her used floss string into the trash can.

"Um, is there soap in there?" Angela asked, glancing quickly at Sharon.

"There's never soap," Sharon said coldly. She rinsed her mouth and hands, wiped them with a brown paper towel, and turned to leave.

Angela was almost grateful. She wanted to talk to Sharon, but she didn't know what to say anymore. Should she tell her she was planning to go to Let's Bolt that night? No. Sharon would only tell her not to go. Was there any point telling her about the dumb conversation between her and Jordan the night before? Or discussing the yearbook theme? Or anything?

When Sharon was halfway to the door, she stopped and turned around, facing Angela. "So, I just think you should know what people are saying about you."

"What," Angela said.

"That you think you're so *above* everyone now. And that Rayanne Graff is like God to you, and you just do whatever she says," Sharon continued. "She's just using you. Like she did Jodie Barsh. I just thought you should know."

Angela looked at Sharon. "What about Jodie Barsh? What did Rayanne do?"

"Oh, please." Sharon rolled her eyes. "It's, like, *so known*."

Angela didn't know what Sharon was talking about. She didn't really care, either. Rayanne had had her own life before being friends with her. Just like Angela had been friends with Sharon. *Had.*

"So tell me what I did, Angela. I mean, I would really like to know." Sharon's bottom lip quivered.

"Nothing!" Angela cried. "It's not—"

"So you just drop your oldest friend for no reason?" Sharon asked. "What did I *do*?"

"Nothing. I mean, it isn't like one thing, it's not like that," Angela insisted, feeling helpless to explain herself.

Sharon folded her arms across her chest. "So. Fine. Just, like...never speak to me again. Real *mature*, Angela."

Something in Angela's throat crinkled. It was the feeling she always got right before she started crying. She had this picture in her mind of her and Sharon, running down the stairs at her house, laughing and shrieking. That would never happen again. And it had only been a few months ago. It was this part of her life that was completely over. "But I *want* to speak to you. I never..." Her voice wavered.

Sharon shook her head. "Forget it." She bit her lip and stared at Angela. "So, your hair? Did Patty, like, hemorrhage when she saw it?"

Angela started to smile. "Almost." She risked a glance

at Sharon. Maybe they could find a way to stay friends. Or at least to be decent to each other.

"I have to say…" Sharon glanced into Angela's eyes. "I hate it," she said. Then she left the bathroom.

Angela felt as if her heart had turned to that vaguely butterscotch pudding she'd eaten for lunch. She looked at her face in the mirror and touched her copper-red hair.

Sharon was acting like Angela had a choice in the matter. When someone like Rayanne came into your life, you just accepted that things were going to change. Drastically. For better or for worse. But mostly because they had to change, or you were going to stay stuck at fifteen forever.

Which was a fate even worse than death, or yearbook. Like a car warranty, fifteen years or fifteen thousand miles of boredom…whichever came first.

"Well, I guess it's just us girls at home tonight," Angela's mother said that night at dinner. She looked at Angela's father, who was sitting silently at the other end of the table. He said nothing, and Mrs. Chase simply shrugged.

"Mom? At home? What does that mean—I'm grounded? Just because of last night?" Angela asked. "But Rayanne invited me to sleep over tonight. And it *is* a Friday." She made a show of slicing off a big hunk of pot roast. Maybe if she ate more, her parents wouldn't get so suspicious.

"Rayanne? That girl from the other day? The one who devoured an entire pound of my cheese?" Mrs. Chase looked horrified.

"Mom, she likes cheese, she was hungry," Angela said, setting down her fork. "Does that make her a bad person? You're ruling out, like, half the people in the world."

"Or at least Wisconsin," her father added, smiling.

"Mom, I want to watch a movie tonight," Danielle, Angela's ten-year-old little sister, announced.

Mrs. Chase looked exasperated. "Listen, I've seen this Rayanne person exactly once. I don't know her or her parents—"

"What? You never spent the night at a friend's house?" Angela's father teased her.

"Mom, you *offered* her the cheese," Angela argued. "And stop calling her 'this Rayanne *person*.' And anyway, you don't even have to drive me. Rickie's cousin—"

"Graham, you haven't even met this Rickie yet," her mother said to her father.

"Stop calling everyone '*this* Rayanne' and '*this* Rickie'!" Angela cried. "It's *so* incredibly patronizing."

"I'm sorry. It's just that I find..." Mrs. Chase paused, as if holding herself back. "I find Rickie...a little confusing."

"Okay, so he's bi," Angela said.

"Bi?" her mother repeated.

"It means bisexual," Danielle said.

"What?!" exclaimed her mother. "Graham, did you hear that?"

"Who cares what he is?" Angela fired back before her father could say a word. "His cousin can still drive a *car*!" Tossing her napkin onto the table, Angela ran upstairs to her room. This was definitely not going the way she'd planned. Why did everyone have to make such a big deal about Rayanne and Rickie? So they weren't as "normal" as Sharon or her. So they didn't have these neat, easy families. Since when was being bi or liking cheddar a crime?

Really, Mom. You are so limited. Angela grabbed the bag of clothes that Rayanne had given her to wear to Let's Bolt.

As she came down the stairs, both her parents were standing at the bottom, waiting for her. "So is this girl's mother going to be there?" Mrs. Chase asked.

"No, Mom. *This girl* Rayanne lives by her wits in an alley," Angela said flatly. "Yes, obviously! They live in the same place! Obviously her mother is going to be there!"

Was that too obviously defensive?

"Okay. Fine. Go spend the night at some total stranger's house. I don't care," her mother said.

"Oh, like you mean that!" Angela exclaimed. She could just see her mother holding that against her for weeks to come, no matter how smoothly the night went.

"I do. Go!" She turned to Angela's father. "And you, go shoot pool with your brother, or wherever it is you're going!"

Angela slipped through the door and leaned against it, relieved she was out of the house, angry at her mother, and...confused. What was that last remark supposed to mean? Her father was obviously going to play pool with her Uncle Neil. Where else would he go?

But she didn't have time to think about it now. She slipped into the bushes on her front lawn; she had just enough time to change into her outfit before Rayanne, Rickie, and Rickie's cousin showed.

"Hey, Chase!"

Angela froze, her shirt pulled halfway over her head. "Get out of here, Krakow!"

"Uh, you're breaking, like, fourteen different laws right now," Brian said.

Angela finished changing, pulled Rayanne's black

miniskirt down a quarter inch, and stepped out from behind the cluster of bushes. Brian was holding a flannel shirt she'd tossed aside. When he saw her, he dropped it onto the ground. Angela quickly picked it up and stuffed it into her bag with the rest of her clothes. She might want it later, if it got cold.

"You looked better before," Brian commented, following her on his bike down to the street.

Angela sighed. "Like I'm devastated."

"Like *I* am."

Angela stopped under a streetlight and fiddled with her compact. The fluorescent glare made her face look yellow-gray in the tiny mirror.

"Oh, look at me," sneered Brian. "I'm way cool. I'm off with my way-cool friends to sniff floor wax. Who are you waiting for? Catalano?"

How does someone like Brian Krakow even know that someone like Jordan Catalano exists? They barely even share the same city. "I'm going to Let's Bolt. Not that you'd even know what that is—"

"Like they're really going to let you into Let's Bolt," Brian scoffed, coasting around Angela on his banana bike seat as she walked up to the end of the block. He turned right and she turned left.

"Quit it!" Angela cried, almost crashing into Brian as he circled back toward her. The last thing she needed was bicycle grease on Rayanne's clothes. That wasn't exactly the look she had in mind.

"Angela, you're not stupid, so don't act like it, okay? It's a stupid act!" Brian said.

A large, old American car pulled up in front of them. "Everybody is an act, Krakow. Including you," Angela said, opening the rear door of the car.

"So have a really amazing night. Okay, I'm going to throw up now, have a wonderful—"

Angela slammed the door. "My neighbor," she explained to everyone in the car. "My clueless neighbor." She glanced out the back window and saw Brian standing all alone in the middle of the street, the streetlight reflecting off the bike's fat metal handlebars.

"You look so tough, I can't stand it!" Rayanne cried. "This is going to be one amazing night."

"Where's Tino?" Rickie asked about an hour later. They were sitting on a curb outside of Let's Bolt, an old brick factory that used to be Willet's Nut and Bolt, only the building had been abandoned in the sixties and the sign had faded a long time ago.

"He'll be here, okay? God, you're so impatient." Rayanne pulled a bottle of whiskey out of the inside pocket of her black leather jacket. She took a swig and passed the bottle to Rickie. "Haven't you ever waited for anything before?"

Rickie stared at the bottle, then passed it to Angela. "Yeah, for my life to start."

Angela held the whiskey bottle in front of her, examining it. Just how strong was this stuff, she wondered. She'd never had any before. Any whiskey. Any liquor. Any anything. Never even a sip of wine or beer at home with her parents. No sneaking down to the liquor cabinet. Rickie's comment about waiting for his life to start was making a lot of sense. She lifted the bottle to her lips and took a small sip.

Instant chaos. Her throat felt like it had just made contact with a blowtorch. She struggled not to make a face, to take it as coolly as Rayanne had.

"If you were about to do it? What would you want the person to say? Right before," Rickie asked.

Rayanne took another swig of whiskey. "How about—'This won't take long.'" She laughed and raised the bottle high.

"No, seriously," Rickie pleaded.

"'Don't I know you from somewhere?'" Rayanne continued, wiping her mouth and laughing even louder.

"Come on." Rickie sounded frustrated. "For real. Like...romantic."

Angela gazed up at the night sky. "'You're so beautiful, it hurts to look at you.'"

Nobody responded for a few seconds. Then Rayanne said, sounding incredulous, "'It hurts to *look* at you'? Like...where would it hurt?" She snickered.

"I really like that. How did you think of that?" Rickie asked, gazing at Angela with utter admiration in his dark brown eyes. Angela shrugged.

Rayanne jumped up and started running away, through the parking lot. "I'm telling Jordan!" she cried.

"No—wait—Ray*anne*!" Angela chased her, running as fast as she could in the platform shoes that Rayanne had lent her.

"Jordan!" Rayanne shrieked, half doubled over with laughter as she ran ahead of Angela. "Angela says—"

Suddenly Rayanne reeled backward a few steps. She had crashed right into two older-looking guys who'd just walked out of the club. "Hey!" Rayanne said, making a quick recovery. "Can you get us in?"

"How old are you, anyway?" one of them asked. His black hair was slicked back, and he was wearing a black leather jacket.

Rayanne turned to look at Angela, and they both

cracked up laughing. Rickie jogged to a stop behind them.

"So...you want to go somewhere?" the first guy asked.

Angela stopped laughing. This guy seriously wanted to *go* somewhere with them? Like...where? What did he think would actually happen? He looked like he was in his twenties.

"Do you?" Rayanne asked Angela.

"I don't know," Angela said slowly. *Not really*.

"If they're really young, is that, like, kidnapping or something?" the second guy asked.

"What do you think, Rickie?" Rayanne asked. "You wanna go?"

"Hey. Not three." The guy with the slicked-back hair pointed to Rayanne, and then Angela. "You, and you."

"I'm not leaving Rickie here!" Angela protested.

"Rickie don't mind," Rayanne practically slurred.

"I don't mind," Rickie said softly, shrugging.

Angela looked at him. Was he just saying that? If she had her way, she'd rather stay with Rickie than go anywhere with these two guys. She didn't like the way the first guy kept staring at her. She crossed her arms in front of her.

"Hey, you. Come over here," the first guy said to Rayanne, who'd backed up a few steps. "I want to ask you something."

"Ask me from there," Rayanne replied.

"I want to ask you over here," he repeated.

"Come on, man, they're too young," the other guy warned.

Rayanne tilted the bottle to her lips as she

approached the first guy, who had moved to stand over by his van. "I don't take orders, and I'm not stupid."

"Oh yeah? You came when I called you," he pointed out.

Angela felt her heart start to beat faster. *Something is actually about to happen,* she thought. *But it's...too actual.*

Rayanne gave him a challenging look. She put her leg up on the side of the van, and before Angela could even blink, the guy had grabbed Rayanne and turned her around. He was leaning against her, pressing her back against the van...touching her.

"Let go of her! Leave her alone!" Angela rushed up behind him and pounded on his shoulders.

"What's *your* problem?" He threw Rayanne to the ground.

Angela went to help Rayanne up, reaching out for her arm, but Rayanne pulled away. "I can take care of myself!" she yelled, tossing the whiskey bottle at the van. It shattered into a million pieces.

"Oh, man, you are *dead*!" the first guy threatened.

"Forget it, let's just go!" his friend urged, pulling him away.

Rickie leaned close to Angela as Rayanne crawled to her feet. "She won't remember this tomorrow," he said softly. "She blacks out when she drinks. I gotta go."

Rickie took off just as a police car showed up, as if it had been waiting out in the alley for something like this to happen. Which, Angela reflected, was probably true. Rickie disappeared, the guys took off, and Angela and Rayanne were left staring at two policemen.

I take it all back. I don't want my life to start, Angela

thought desperately, biting her lip. *I want to be good and boring and stay home on Friday nights with my mother and little sister drinking hot chocolate and—*

"Relax. We're not going to arrest you," the younger-looking officer said. "Just get into the car, please. We'll escort you home."

Angela smiled. *Well. In that case, I take back what I just said.*

"Could you do the siren, please?" Rayanne begged as she slid into the backseat. "Pleeeaaassse?" she slurred, looking out at the older officer, who was about to help Angela into the car. "Oh my God!" Rayanne shrieked, her eyes widening. "Angela, look!"

Angela turned and glanced over her shoulder. There, walking under the spotlight outside the club's door, was Jordan Catalano. Hearing Rayanne's voice, he looked over in their direction, his eyes struggling to make them out in the darkness.

"Angela?" he called.

Oh my God. He actually knows my name.

The police officer slammed the door closed, just as Angela heard Jordan call to his friends, "Hey, I know that girl!"

As the police car pulled out of the parking lot, Angela couldn't help smiling. Sure, she was in trouble. But Jordan had actually recognized her. Like, in public.

"I knew what I was doing back there. You know," Rayanne said as the police car headed down the street.

"Okay," Angela said.

Rayanne smiled, her eyes nearly closing. "I'll always watch out for you. Okay? I'll always be there for you. So don't worry."

"I won't," Angela said, carefully studying Rayanne's

face. She looked so young and sweet, with her head resting against the seat, as if she were simply taking a nap in the back of her parents' car on a long road trip. As if nothing that had just happened could even be possible.

Jordan knows who I am, Angela considered again, turning to look out the window at the quickly passing city blocks. Things were changing in her life. Something was actually happening. *Finally*.

Chapter 3

"Right. Like you're not going to tell me what happened. Chase!" Brian started following Angela down the street. He'd been up in a tree, reading, when the police car pulled up in front of Angela's house. *As if that doesn't sum up Brian's life, like...in an acorn shell. I'm out at Let's Bolt, getting hit on, and he's in an oak tree with a flashlight, studying biology.*

"Oh. These guys started hitting on us," Angela said breezily.

"What, like sexual harassment?" Brian looked shocked.

"No. Like...guys," Angela explained. She stepped carefully down the sidewalk, still feeling awkward in Rayanne's shoes. She didn't want to go into her house right away.

"So. We picked a theme for the yearbook," Brian announced. "You want to take a walk?"

"Brian, we *are* taking a walk," Angela said, irritated.

"Okay."

"Just don't always *say* everything," Angela told him. "So. Who told you I like Jordan Catalano?"

"Nobody," Brian said. "So listen...Angela?"

She stopped, staring straight ahead. Her father was standing on the street, under a dim streetlight. He was leaning against a shiny dark green sports car, talking with a woman Angela had never seen before—a young woman—and he was leaning up close to her, like every word she said mattered to him. A lot. *But he said he was playing pool...with Uncle Neil...*

Her mother's words suddenly echoed in her head. *"Or wherever it is you're going."*

Angela turned abruptly and walked in the opposite direction. Brian hurried after her. When she turned to go up the sidewalk to her house, she tripped on a twig, stumbling, almost crashing to the ground.

Brian grabbed her arm, steadying her.

"These aren't my shoes," Angela explained.

"It's The Year Two Thousand," Brian said quickly. "That's the theme. Just...what it will be like." Angela could feel him looking at her, watching her carefully, waiting for her to break. "Angela..."

She brushed her dirt-covered hands against Rayanne's miniskirt. "I have to go in."

"Okay," Brian agreed.

She started to walk up the driveway, then stopped and turned to Brian. "That's a pathetic theme."

He shrugged. "I know."

Angela went into the house and leaned against the closed door. Everything was very quiet. She crept upstairs to her bedroom and quickly changed into a T-shirt and shorts. She washed her face very carefully, taking off all the heavy black eyeliner Rayanne had put on earlier, in the car. Before the whole awful night started.

She stared at her reflection in the mirror for a few minutes, at her new red hair, at her bloodshot eyes. They matched.

On her way back to her bedroom, Angela stopped in the hallway. Then she went into her mother's room and just stood in the doorway, watching her mother write a check and stuff it into an envelope.

"What happened to spending the night?" Patty Chase asked without looking up.

Angela shrugged.

"Did you at least have fun?"

"Sort of," Angela said. *Until I got home, anyway.* She stared at the side of the bed where her father always slept, at the flatly pressed sheets. She pictured him standing outside, just one block away, with another woman, while her mother was here, waiting for him, all alone. "I'm really sorry," she managed to get out before she started to cry. "About my hair...and everything."

Her mother held out her arms. Angela crawled onto the bed next to her...where her father was supposed to be.

"It's not important. It'll grow out," her mother said, smoothing Angela's hair. "It actually looks okay. In my humble opinion."

Angela felt her whole body relax, her face pressed against the pillow, her feet tucked under the afghan at the end of the bed. *Just like when I was little,* she thought. *And I couldn't sleep, or I was scared of the dark, and I came in here.*

So maybe everything hasn't changed.

*   *   *

"Hi."

"Hi," Angela said, shocked that Jordan Catalano was actually talking to her.

"Out on bail?"

"Yeah. So how was your weekend?"

"Sucked." Jordan leaned against the wall and closed his eyes.

Angela stared at his mouth, the way his lips curved slightly at the corners. If only—

Jordan opened his eyes. "Gotta go."

He looked at her, and seemed about to smile. Then he walked away.

Angela sat in science class, staring at a diagram of a pig heart, replaying the entire minute-long conversation in her head. She knew she had to get beyond this, to at least turn these moments into *two*-minute conversations. But she didn't know how. She'd only been kissed three times before, in randomly strange situations. She'd never had a boyfriend. How was she supposed to do all those things that got you from point A (Alone) to point B (Boyfriend)? Was there a chart? Some kind of diagram she could refer to?

"You have got to progress to the next phase of this," Rayanne had told her that morning. "Think of me and Rickie. How much more can we take?"

"I just don't want to look like I'm throwing myself at him," Angela said in self-defense.

"Excuse me? People throwing themselves at other people? Is, like, the basis of civilization," Rayanne argued.

But when Jordan was around, Angela turned into the weakest version of herself. She'd try to talk, but her mind and her mouth weren't connected at all. Like that morning. Her trying to throw herself at him turned into "How was your weekend?" *Why didn't I just say, "Have a nice day, and thanks for shopping here!"*

"Now, to review." Ms. Chavatal dropped a heart on Sharon's desk.

She's actually walking around the class, handing out hearts, Angela thought, sickened. *And she expects us to...touch them. Dissect them. Or whatever.*

"What are the elements of a true experiment? An experiment must test a...*what?*" Ms. Chavatal asked.

"A hypothesis," said Brian, sitting beside Angela. They were lab partners.

"And a hypothesis consists of several...what?" Ms. Chavatal dumped a heart on Brian's desk. Angela stared at it, expecting it to start beating at any moment and drop off the desk onto the floor. Her stomach turned. Why a pig heart? What gave them the right to poke around some poor pig's heart? What about Wilbur? Hadn't anyone on the school board ever read *Charlotte's Web?*

Brian gave her a concerned look, his lips pressed together. Angela frowned at him. It wasn't that she couldn't *handle* it. She just didn't want to. Handle it. Like, physically.

"A hypothesis consists of several assumptions. And true experimentation depends on...what?"

Angela heard someone in the hallway outside the open door. "Psst. Psst." She looked over and saw Rayanne, gesturing to her. Rickie was standing behind Rayanne waving.

With a quick glance at Ms. Chavatal, who was handing out latex gloves, Angela slid out of her seat and ran out of the room.

"Jordan Catalano is making you a fake I.D. And he's

going to bring it to you tonight. You can thank me now, or later," Rayanne calmly informed Angela once they were in the girls' room.

"Oh my God…"

"Hey, I did it for you, okay? It's a good thing!" Rayanne insisted.

"I bet people can actually die of embarrassment. I bet it's been medically proven," Angela said. Rayanne had actually talked to Jordan *about* her…like, as a subject.

"Hey, worst-case scenario: You get a fake I.D., which you need anyway. Right?" Rayanne asked.

"Just…wait a second. Tell me everything he said. How did he act? Did he seem bored, or did he—"

"He flopped uncontrollably to the ground, okay? Rickie had to hold down his tongue," Rayanne said.

"And I wasn't even there," Rickie said.

Angela laughed, embarrassed. So maybe everyone didn't keep track of other people so intensely, or want to know every single word that was said during a conversation so they could replay it in their head for hours afterward.

When the bell rang, Angela, Rickie, and Rayanne walked out of the girls' room to head for the cafeteria.

"Hey, Chase!"

Angela turned and saw Brian walking toward her. *What I, like, dread? Is when people who know you in completely different ways end up in the same place. And it's like: Which you do you act like?*

"Thanks for leaving me a whole heart to dissect and clean up," Brian said, glancing at Rickie and Rayanne.

You have to develop this combination you. On the spot.

Angela smiled weakly. She didn't really care about helping Brian, not when it involved biological science.

Sure, he'd been nice to her the other night, but he was still Brian Krakow.

"So, Chavatal thinks we're both working on my volumeter for extra credit," Brian continued.

"Your what?" Rickie raised one eyebrow.

"It's this experiment," Angela explained. "There's, like, a mouse involved, I think..."

Rayanne took a step closer to Brian. "What's your name again?"

"Look, I already executed the entire apparatus," Brian went on, ignoring Rayanne.

"The *apparatus*?" Rayanne giggled.

"So I think the least you could do is help me work on it, because I've done most of the work and you're getting credit. So, tomorrow night—"

"He wants you to work on his *apparatus*," Rayanne said. "And you know what that means."

"Just shut up, okay?" Brian glared at her.

Rayanne gasped. "But what would your *parents* say?"

"My parents are out of town. Which has nothing to do with...it doesn't...I mean..." Brian stammered.

"She'll be there," Rayanne said.

"Rayanne!" Angela cried. She did not want to help Brian at his house with any kind of apparatus. Especially if his parents weren't there. Not that he would do anything. It was just very uncomfortable, that was all.

Rayanne tugged at Angela's sleeve, and they stepped aside. "It's perfect," she whispered. "You can meet Jordan there."

Angela started laughing, then realized that Rayanne was *serious*. "Jordan Catalano?" she whispered. "At Brian Krakow's house? It's, like, against the laws of nature."

"Chase! Are you going to help me or not?" Brian demanded.

Rayanne looked at Angela, raising both eyebrows. "No, it's going to be you and Jordan. Alone."

"Oh God," Angela gasped. "Yeah, I'll be there!" she called to Brian.

"Good. Because you will be getting extra credit," Brian said.

Rickie peered at Brian. "Is extra credit, like, your whole life?"

Brian turned and walked away.

"Okay, how is this supposed to, like, actually work?" Angela asked. "How does Jordan end up *dropping by* the Krakows'?"

"Don't worry. I got you this far, right?" Rayanne asked.

"Oh. Hi."

Angela couldn't believe how long it had been since she'd been inside Brian Krakow's house. She used to spend tons of time there when she was little. She and Brian used to play together constantly.

It smells exactly the same. Sort of a mixture of macaroni and cheese and Mr. Clean. Which is reassuring and annoying at the same time. Kind of like Brian himself.

"That mouse can breathe in there, right?" She stared at the volumeter on the round kitchen table.

"Of course," Brian said, sitting down at the table.

Angela paced around the linoleum floor, stopping to brush some crumbs off the counter into the sink and to adjust the magnets on the refrigerator. *Why do I care what this place looks like? It's not even my house.* "So, listen. Rayanne and Rickie are dropping by later. To bring me something. No big deal." She turned to Brian and took a deep breath. *Don't hate me. Because I almost hate myself, and if you did, too, that would, like, put me over the top. Or is it the bottom?*

"I knew you wouldn't be much help," Brian said critically. He jotted something down in his lab notebook.

Angela continued pacing. After about ten minutes, she sat down opposite Brian and stared at the mouse in the volumeter, wondering how it must feel to have your pressure measured...and then written about, to prove a point.

Rayanne and Rickie pounded at the door a few minutes later, and walked right into the house. "Look, I know this is your house, but could you leave for a second?" Rayanne asked Brian.

"Oh. So you actually admit that it's my house. Because I was wondering," Brian said. "The way you just, like, walked in and everything."

"I'm not saying leave the house. Leave the kitchen," Rayanne urged.

"Come on, we can talk in here," Angela said, standing and moving into the dining room. She peeked through the lace curtain on the window. Jordan's large red Plymouth convertible was parked outside with the top up, and she could vaguely make out the shape of his head in the front seat. Not just his head, like it was decapitated, but all of him. In the flesh. Sitting there, waiting for *her.*

"Are you going out there or what?" Rayanne demanded, cracking her gum.

"See, there's thinking about him, right? Which is what I do. All the time," Angela confessed. "It's like an—"

"Obsession," Rickie interjected.

"Right." Rayanne shrugged. "So?"

"So it keeps me going. Like I need that, to get through the day, because—"

"It's an obsession!" Rickie added again.

"Right!" Angela said, glad that somebody understood. "And if you make it real? It's not the same. It's not yours anymore. So I don't know what to do, because maybe if I ruin it tonight, maybe I'd be better off just having the *fantasy* of Jordan Catalano."

Rickie smiled. "I completely understand."

"Well, I completely disagree," Rayanne said. "You want Jordan Catalano. In actuality. Like, the body *and* the fantasy."

Angela peeked out the window again. Jordan was now leaning against his car, smoking a cigarette. While she watched, he took a final drag, then tossed the cigarette butt on the ground and crushed it with the heel of his suede sneaker. Then he opened the door and started getting into the car.

He's about to leave, Angela realized. *And Rayanne's right*.

"Hi." Angela leaned her hands against the passenger door's open window. "So...I have the money. And...you have my I.D. Right?"

Jordan shrugged, pushing his hair up over the collar of his brown corduroy jacket. "Yeah."

"So this is your car?" Angela asked. She wasn't sure how much harder she could actually *try* to make conversation without pulling a muscle.

"Get in," Jordan said.

Angela laughed nervously. "I...um...I can't. I mean, I should stay here. So I can't, like, go anywhere. It's extra credit."

"Huh?" Jordan seemed stunned, as if no girl had ever refused him before.

"It's a long story," Angela said with a wave of her hand. "But the point is I can't go."

Jordan looked at her, puzzled. "I didn't say *go* anywhere."

"Oh, okay." Angela opened the heavy door and got into the car. She turned to Jordan, but he was staring straight ahead at the street. So she did the same thing. And waited. *Now what?*

Jordan didn't say anything. Angela stared intently at the leaves slowly drifting off the huge oak tree in front of her house and clutched the leather seat with her fingernails. She was about to try to say something when Jordan suddenly leaned over in front of her—across her—in her lap, practically.

Angela pressed her back against the seat, afraid of being too close, of seeming to make any kind of move. Jordan opened the glove compartment, pulled out a phony I.D. card, and handed it to Angela.

She slowly took the card from him. He was looking into her eyes. He was so...gorgeous. He was so...*close*. If he were any closer, he would be out of focus.

What's amazing is when you can actually feel your life going somewhere. Like your life just figured out how to get good.

Angela was actually staring into Jordan Catalano's eyes. And it wasn't a fantasy. It was almost too much to take. She looked down at her new I.D. "Wow, it looks real. Wait, why does this have yesterday's date—"

Jordan suddenly lunged forward, clumsily pressing his lips against hers.

Angela pushed at his chest with her hands. "Hey!"

Jordan backed off, sliding back to his side of the car.

"Sorry, it's just that I was *talking*," Angela said.

"Whatever," Jordan said, like he didn't care whether she wanted to kiss him or not.

Angela shook her head. So far this was turning out to be even more weird than she'd expected. The only thing she could think to do was discuss the I.D. He had gotten it for her, after all, so it was the whole point of their even being together in the same car. "So, how come it says—"

Jordan leaned over, and before Angela could move, he was kissing her again, this time more harshly. She pushed him back, and his head knocked against the rearview mirror.

"Quit it!" Angela said, rubbing her jaw. "I mean, you have to work up to that. I don't open that wide at the *dentist*."

Jordan adjusted the mirror. "How old are you?"

"I don't believe this. What's your point?" She stared at Jordan. "Fifteen!"

"You act younger," Jordan said.

There's nothing worse than being called younger...when you're already, like, too young. But who was Jordan Catalano to tell her how old she was? At least she hadn't been a sophomore for three years running. You tended to stay young when you knocked down your school years in order.

"First of all? You don't know me well enough to say how old I seem," Angela told him angrily. "And second—"

"You talk a lot," Jordan commented.

"Excuse me? I've said, like, eight sentences to you,

total, in my entire life!" Angela cried.

Jordan let out a long, loud, bored-sounding sigh. "This whole day has been one long thing that doesn't make any sense."

Tell me about it, Angela thought. Jordan leaned back in his seat, resting his head against it. He closed his eyes, and for a second, he looked so peaceful. Angela had never seen him that close before. He wasn't doing or saying anything, and she still wanted to watch him, look at him…memorize him, maybe. Part of his sleeve was touching her elbow. Then everything started to seem perfect, like this was how it was meant to happen.

This is the perfect moment for him to kiss me. For him to anything me.

Jordan opened his eyes. He sat up straighter and leaned toward her, coming closer…like he was going to use the glove compartment move again…but this time Angela was ready for him. Jordan reached across her and put his hand on—

The door handle.

"Well, I gotta go. So…" He pulled the handle back and the door opened.

Angela nodded and got out of the car in a daze. He gunned the motor and peeled off down the street.

She just stood there on the curb, thinking, *I could kill him right now. With my bare hands.*

After a few minutes, she went back inside the Krakows' house. Rickie and Rayanne were putting their coats on, getting ready to leave. Brian was standing in the middle of the kitchen, staring at the mess they had made: crushed tortilla chips, cheese dip spilled on the counter, six half-empty cans of soda.

"I'm not going to take the extra credit," Angela told

Brian, turning the water on to wet a sponge. The least she could do was help him clean up.

"Whatever," Brian said.

"So your mother and I went ballroom dancing. It's harder than it sounds," Angela's father said when she got home about half an hour later. He was sitting at the kitchen table in his robe, reading the newspaper.

Fascinating, Dad. But I'd rather think about killing Jordan Catalano right now, if that's okay.

"Dad, I don't feel like talking. No offense," she replied. *But I just can't get that image of you and that woman out of my head whenever I see you.* She took a plastic container of leftover spaghetti out of the refrigerator and waited for him to leave.

"Who, me? I don't want to talk," her father said. "Certainly not to you. It's just...well, how did your experiment go?" He stood up and walked over to the counter.

"Experiment?" Angela repeated.

"With Brian?"

"Oh." Angela shrugged. "He did most of it."

"So was this, like...a date?"

"With Brian Krakow? No!" Angela could not imagine a worse way to spend the night. Except maybe exchanging lame kisses with Jordan. "Anyway, we don't, like, have dates. People just hang out together. In a bunch."

"Oh." Her father nodded. "So then was someone else there? Someone that you like?"

The bell on the microwave went off. *It's so strange how parents can turn psychic. Like, out of nowhere, come up with the right answer.*

"I was just wondering. You don't have to tell me,"

her father said. "It's okay to like someone. But boys your age can sometimes...I don't know."

"Dad, *I* know," Angela said, twirling her fork around several strands of spaghetti. But maybe she didn't. "Can sometimes what?"

"You know. Not know how to act. Or who to be. Or how to be what you want them to be. Does that make any sense?" He looked nervously at her.

Angela nodded.

"Okay. Well, uh. See you later." Her father went upstairs. Angela put her dish in the sink and followed him. After changing into her nightshirt, she realized she was absolutely dying of thirst. She went down to the kitchen to get a glass of milk.

When she got halfway down, she could hear her father talking to somebody on the phone. He was speaking very quietly, like it was a secret. And Angela knew instantly that it had to be the woman from the other night. Because he wouldn't whisper at ten o'clock to his brother Neil, or anyone else.

"It's just...I'm sorry," she heard her father say. "I can't do this. I'm sorry. Okay, good-bye."

Angela walked into the kitchen just as her father was hanging up the phone. He looked nervous, but not guilty, about being caught. *"I can't do this,"* Angela repeated in her head. Did that mean that nothing had ever really happened? And why did she have to see these things, and overhear these things? She almost wished she didn't know anything about it.

Like her mother, maybe.

"Don't stay up too late," her father said, nodding at her as he passed. "You're going to have a hard time getting up tomorrow morning."

When he was gone, Angela walked over to the napkin holder, where she'd stashed her fake I.D. *I have to say...that makes me feel better about men. In general. Not...like...my dad has anything in common with Jordan Catalano, but still.*

She felt like she had her father back. And part of herself, too, because he was part of her identity.

She stared at her new I.D. She was from Montana now. Her name was Christy Smith. And she was exactly one day old. If only it were that easy to just change everything about yourself.

She wondered if Jordan knew he got the date wrong. She wasn't born yesterday. And she definitely acted her age. In fact, Rayanne once told her she ought to be listed in the dictionary under the definition of fifteen.

Or did she say the poster child for fifteen? Maybe it was both.

Anyway, Jordan didn't know anything about her. He had no right to say how old or young she seemed. *Couldn't he tell that I was, like, ready to be whatever he wanted me to be?*

Chapter 4

Angela Chase and Jordan Catalano.
Complete Sex !!! In his car.
Can you believe her?

Angela stared at the note as a toilet flushed. She and
Rayanne were hanging in the girls' room the next day,
between classes. "Who would write a note like this?"

"Everyone writes notes like that. *We* write notes like
that," Rayanne reminded her, perched on top of the radiator.

"Yeah, maybe. But we only write notes that are
true," Angela argued.

Rayanne frowned. "This isn't true?"

"Rayanne! We barely made out. You haven't been
telling people—"

Rickie walked into the girls' room. "So, what's this I
hear about you and Jordan?"

Angela leaned back against the tiled wall. "I can't believe this!"

"Angela, you have to start thinking about this as a positive thing. It could help you get to the next level with Jordan," Rayanne argued, hopping off the radiator.

"I thought the I.D. was supposed to do that," Angela said, folding her arms across her chest and giving Rayanne an accusing look.

"You kissed him, didn't you? I mean, didn't he at least think you were a good kisser?"

Angela felt her face turn red. "I don't know!"

"Well, did you like how *he* kissed?" Rickie asked.

Angela shrugged. "They weren't the kind of kisses you could actually evaluate. They were more like...introductory kisses."

"There's no such thing." Rayanne shook her head. "You're crazy. You **sh**ould have had sex with him."

Maybe I would have, Angela thought. *If I knew anything about anything.* Rayanne made no secret of the fact that she'd slept with different guys, but for Angela it was different. In comparison to Rayanne, she *was*, like...born yesterday. Or at least last week. Not that she didn't think about sex. But she didn't know when she would actually start having it.

"Introductory kisses," Rickie mused. "Is that like a class I could get into?"

"There. Did you see that?" Angela asked Rayanne while they waited for gym to start. A boys' gym class was just finishing a basketball game, and now they were practicing lay-ups. Each time one of the guys did a lay-up, he stopped and smiled at Angela before running back to the end of the line.

"People are *looking* at me," Angela complained.

Rayanne shrugged. "Good."

"No, they're *looking* at me," Angela insisted.

A senior Angela vaguely recognized as being the captain of some team did a lay-up, then walked over toward her and stopped. "Hi." He grinned.

"Hi," Angela said.

He smiled even wider, then turned and jogged back to the class.

"See? Do you *see* what I'm talking about?" Angela asked.

"He said 'Hi,'" Rayanne replied calmly.

"That wasn't 'Hi.' That was a different 'Hi.'"

"Like...he-wants-to-get-to-know-you-better 'Hi,'" Rayanne said.

"Right. From someone who never talks to me, has never talked to me, doesn't even know who I am—"

"He does now," Rayanne said. "I told you the note was good." She grinned.

"Rayanne!" Angela cried. Her attention was temporarily diverted as, across the gym on another basketball court, Jordan faked past two defenders and did a lay-up. He was the kind of person who could get away with never wearing the required clothes for gym. Everyone else had to wear shorts, but he could play in jeans.

Rayanne followed her gaze. "Maybe Jordan started the rumor," she said softly.

"Come on. I doubt it," Angela said. "Why would he?"

Rayanne shrugged. "Well, it *is* a very guy thing to do."

Angela considered it for a minute. For as far back as she could remember, the boys she went to school with had started rumors. In first grade, there was the one about spaghetti being brains. Then in fourth grade a boy had started a rumor that Mrs. Kaposki was actually Mr. Kaposki, just because she had a mustache in need of some serious bleach. And when Sharon started wearing a bra, it was common knowledge that it was a 40D, when it was actually more like a 32B—at least back then, in fifth grade.

But why would someone like Jordan Catalano want people to think he'd had sex with someone like her? Unless it was part of one of those horrible point systems, but she was pretty sure there wasn't anything like that going on at Liberty. So it had to be somebody who actually cared what happened between her and Jordan. But who? As far as she could tell, *she* was the only one who cared. Jordan hadn't even spoken to her since the fake I.D. incident. It was almost as if it had never happened.

"Hi." Suddenly another guy was standing in front of her, grinning at her like he'd just won the lottery.

Almost.

"Honey? Who's Jordan?"

Angela stopped, her hand on the refrigerator door handle. She'd been staring at the shelves, trying to decide what she wanted to drink. "You mean...Jordan Catalano?"

"Is that his last name?" her mother asked.

"I don't know. You brought it up." Angela closed the refrigerator door and turned to her.

"I met Rayanne's mother tonight, after our PTA meeting. She was very excited about you and Rayanne being friends, and also about your new boyfriend, Jordan," her mother said flatly.

"Boyfriend!" Angela practically choked. "That's a laugh."

"So he's not your—"

"Mom, I barely *know* this person," Angela said. Okay, so maybe she knew what his lips felt like when they were pressed against hers, but she still didn't know Jordan Catalano. She didn't know his favorite band, or what he did on weekends, or even his middle name or when his birthday was. And she especially didn't know if he was ever going to be her boyfriend. Not likely, the way things were going since their first non-date.

"So, you and this…Jordan person. You haven't… well, you're not actively—"

It dawned on Angela that the only possible end to that sentence had something to do with sex. She had to interrupt, immediately. "Mom, what did you hear?" she demanded. "What did Rayanne's mom tell you?"

"Nothing." Her mother shrugged. "She didn't tell me anything, really."

"Did she say I was sleeping with Jordan Catalano?" Angela cried. Was it in the newspaper or something? Had somebody posted a sign on the bus stop kiosks? Or was there a general announcement on the radio: The following schools are closed today, it looks like freezing rain, and Angela and Jordan had sex?

"No! She didn't say that. I mean, not in so many words, but—"

"She did tell you! I can't believe this," Angela said angrily. "I cannot believe this. I hate everybody!" She turned and ran out of the kitchen as her parents stared at her, that we're-very-concerned look etched on their faces.

And we didn't have sex! she wanted to scream. Not

that it wasn't obvious, she thought, slamming her bedroom door behind her.

And not that it was anybody's business but hers, if and when they did.

If. She sank onto her bed and hugged her pillow. Maybe the fantasy of Jordan, from afar, was better than the reality of not being with him, up close.

THE UNIVERSAL SIGN OF CHOKING: WHEN A PERSON PUTS A HAND AROUND HIS OR HER THROAT. SEE ILLUSTRATION A.

The next day, Angela found herself staring at the same Heimlich Maneuver chart outside the cafeteria for at least a full minute. She was waiting for Jordan to walk past behind her. She'd seen him coming, like a tornado on the prairie in those old episodes of *Little House*, and she knew she had to get out of the way, hide in the basement, lie in a ditch...do anything except talk to him. What was she supposed to say? "My rumor's fine, how's yours?"

When she sensed Jordan's body moving past her, she waited a minute. Then another. Then she finally turned around.

Jordan was standing right there.

The Heimlich Maneuver would come in handy right about now, Angela thought, resting her hand against her throat. "It's a good thing to know about," she said nervously. "The maneuver and all."

"Yeah! I was just...My uncle choked on a chicken bone once."

Angela laughed. "I'm sorry. I shouldn't laugh. That's a really terrible thing to, like, happen."

"No. It was a turkey bone," Jordan said, looking thoughtful.

So this is what it's like, Angela thought. *We're having an actual conversation. He's talking about poultry bones. And somehow, I know my life will never be the same.*

"Did he survive?" she asked, staring into Jordan's eyes.

Jordan nodded. "Yeah."

All of a sudden Angela knew that the rumor was right. Not in actuality, but in her heart, because at that exact moment she wanted Jordan so much, she would have done anything.

"Look," said Jordan, "I know what people are saying, and I just want you to know that I didn't say anything about...you know."

"I know," Angela said.

"I'm not like that. I don't do that," Jordan went on.

"No." Angela knew that was true, instinctively.

Jordan took a step closer to her. The way he leaned, which was what she'd always loved about him, was the way he was now leaning, his arm on the wall next to her head, his body practically pressed against hers. "It's so weird, huh? The way people talk. I mean, people think we did it," he said softly.

"I know." *And I wish we had.*

"It's like we should have just done it anyway, at this point," Jordan went on.

"Oh?" Was he actually saying what she thought he was saying? Angela felt her heart begin to falter, her body's entire nervous system breaking down. Like her heart was one of those pig hearts, lying on someone's desk, ready for inspection. Analysis: fatal shock.

"I mean, if everybody's talking about it anyway, then maybe we...you know." Jordan leaned even closer, his breath a warm whisper on her ear. "If everybody's assuming it, maybe we should just...maybe..."

It's amazing the things you notice up close. Like the one corner of his collar that's frayed, like he was from a poor family and couldn't afford new shirts. That was all she could focus on, as if her whole world had become that one small, unraveling piece of cotton. "I think I have to go," she said.

"Look, I'm sorry if—"

"No, it's okay," she told Jordan.

"No pressure or anything..."

"No! It's just that I...um...have to go."

"You could think about it." Jordan shrugged.

Angela turned and started walking down the hallway, moving faster and faster with each step, until she turned a corner and, out of sight of Jordan, leaned against the wall to catch her breath. She could not believe what had just happened. What had just almost happened, or what could happen if she only said the word. Or words. Like, "Good idea. Let's go."

It's such a lie that you should do what's in your heart. If we all did what was in our hearts? The world would probably grind to a complete halt.

Jessica Kingfield is a total slut.
Sarah Brooks, ditto.
How about Cynthia Hargrove?
Angela Chase, too.

Angela stared at her name on the wall of the bathroom stall the next day. So, the rumor had been out for less than a week, and she had already made "the wall." She didn't know whether to laugh or cry. It was so *false*. And if it wasn't true about her, then who else was getting slandered? Of course, those other girls *were* kind of sleazy. There was no real argument there.

She was behind the closed stall door, poking through her backpack, looking for her pen, when she heard the door open and two familiar voices start talking.

"But what does that have to do with Angela?" Delia Fisher asked.

"*Because.* That's where it happened—at Brian's house," Sharon said.

"Oh my God. At his *house*?" Delia asked.

"In the front yard," Sharon went on.

Angela desperately wanted to flush the toilet just to drown out their voices. But she had to know.

"Brian watched the whole thing through the kitchen window," Sharon said.

"Wait a second. Why did you hear this from Brian? I thought you and Angela were really tight," Delia said.

"She *was* my best friend, but it's like she's a completely different person now. It's really hard to accept this whole thing. But I know Brian. He wouldn't lie."

I thought I knew Brian, too. Angela uncapped her pen and began scratching blue ink over her name on the flesh-colored metal wall. *But I was wrong.*

"Krakow."

"What?" Brian turned around from the computer in the school library.

"Look, I can't even believe I have to ask you this, but

I have to, so just shut up and listen," Angela said, sliding into the seat next to his. "Why did you lie about me?"

"What?"

"Stop saying that. *'What?'* You *know* what I'm talking about. What you said to Sharon about me and Jordan, and now it's all over school, thanks so much," Angela told him.

"What are you talking about?"

"I heard her, Brian!" Angela said. "You told her terrible things about me—you lied to her."

"I didn't. I mean, I didn't lie, I just suggested...oh, never mind. I can imagine what she did with it." Brian fiddled with the mouse, exiting from one program and going into another. "It's just that you lied too. When you said you didn't know anything about Jordan coming over that night. Because I've thought about it, for, like, fifty hours. You knew it. Didn't you? So you used me."

Angela stared at him. Where was this coming from? "That's not the same as lying—"

"Maybe it is. Because you just did what you wanted, and you didn't care what damage it did, to anyone," Brian said quietly.

"What damage could what I do possibly do to *you*?" Angela asked, confused.

Brian didn't answer.

Maybe Brian had to start the rumor, as a way to get more popular, she thought. Or maybe he was interested in Sharon, and since Sharon wanted to dump on Angela lately, maybe Brian wanted to help by getting on her side.

Or maybe he had no clue about anything, except his volumeter project. And he'd completely ruined her life, with one stupid story about what hadn't happened at his house that night.

I should have known bringing Brian Krakow and Jordan Catalano into the same city block would cause problems. It's just like I told Rayanne—it's against the laws of nature.

She stood up and went out into the hallway, where she practically bumped right into Jordan Catalano. *No*, she thought desperately. *Not now.*

"Angela, could I talk to you a second?" Jordan asked. "How you doing?"

"You know." Angela shrugged. "Life goes on." Sort of.

"Look, uh. I was thinking about what I said to you yesterday. You know, that thing." Jordan shifted on his feet.

"Right. The thing," Angela said slowly.

"Yeah. Look. I'm sorry about that. Afterwards, I thought about it? And I mean, I could see how you got upset."

"I didn't get upset," Angela protested. *More like undone*.

"I mean, you're not like that. So I just wanted to say, you know...I'm sorry," Jordan said.

"No, really, it's okay." *You can talk like that to me whenever you want to.* She searched for a frayed collar, the shape of a bottle of breath freshener in his shirt pocket, anything to hold on to, to focus on. "It wasn't a problem," she told him. "I mean, I did think about it, and I thought maybe what you were saying wasn't so strange because—"

"No, it was really wrong. And so, if you want me to, I'm just going to make it clear that I don't, like, have any real interest in you or anything. So everyone will stop saying that."

All of a sudden, it was like the whole hallway was deserted, and the rest of the world had vanished—and all Angela could hear were those words: *I don't have any real interest in you.* That was the upshot of all of this; that was the truth behind the rumor. Not that it could have been true, the way she thought. But that it could never have been true. Not from Jordan's perspective.

"You know. I'll tell everyone that I barely even know you...which is true," Jordan continued when she didn't respond. "And that, um, basically, we're nothing to each other. And that should solve the problem."

"Solve the problem," Angela repeated. *Nothing to each other.* "Right. Thanks."

"It's the least I can do. You know?"

"Right." Angela nodded.

Jordan shrugged and then turned to walk away. Angela just stood there, watching him slouch from side to side, the tails of his untucked shirt swaying back and forth almost in slow motion. She felt completely destroyed, as if she had just crashed into a wall in a car test and her airbag had failed.

Chapter 5

"So, not to shock you or anything? But your dad's attractive," Rayanne said as she, Angela, and Rickie walked up the front steps of school one morning about a week later.

"Oh, I'm sure," Angela said, shaking her head. *How embarrassing.* Parents didn't *have* good looks, or bad looks. They were older. They had a different set of standards that she didn't really understand. It involved percentages of hair loss and cellulite.

"Not that I'd, you know, attack him or anything. But I wouldn't leave me alone with him either." Rayanne wiggled her eyebrows. "Not for long, anyway."

"Remember when I was leaving yesterday?" Rickie said. "There he was, coming home, right? So I'm like, Hi! And he's like, Hi. And then I'm like, Well, *bye*, and he's—"

"I don't mean just physically. He's nice. You just have a really nice dad, he's really *nice*."

When someone compliments your parents? There's, like,

nothing to say. It's like a stun gun to your brain. But Angela knew that since she was the only one of them whose father was actually still around, Rayanne meant it when she complimented him. She didn't just compliment people for no reason. Insult, yes—compliment, no.

"Plus, his stubble is the perfect length," Rickie commented.

"He doesn't have stubble," Angela protested. "He ran out of razor blades yesterday morning and he was all upset because—"

"Ooh, he gets upset? In-touch-with-his-emotions Dad," Rayanne teased. "I like that in a man."

"Shut up!" Angela cried.

"Just ignore her," Rayanne told Rickie. "Angela can't help herself. She's the product of a two-parent household."

"Yeah. She's practically, like, extinct," Rickie said.

Angela walked through the metal detector into school, handing her backpack to the guard to search. Once she was inside, she saw Kyle and Sharon, making out, right in front of everyone, like they couldn't *control* themselves, almost.

Sharon's life is moving forward in this, like, natural, healthy way, while mine is like... She touched a bump on her chin. *Clogged.* Angela knew that Sharon had met Kyle after one of those big Friday night football games that everyone was supposed to attend. *I'll probably go my whole life and never meet anyone. At any game. Of any size.*

"What is a metamorphosis?" Mr. Renaldi, who was temporarily teaching Angela's English class, waited for an answer. Nobody said anything.

Angela stared at the initials carved into her desk, wondering how much a person had to care about themselves to actually want to leave a permanent mark of their existence behind.

"Brian?" Mr. Renaldi finally prompted.

Brian cleared his throat. "When someone totally changes into something else. Or just...when anything changes shape." He glanced over at Sharon.

Angela couldn't exactly blame Brian for wanting to look at her. It was an amazing transformation. This person that she and Brian had played jacks with was suddenly this...woman. Who could attract seniors.

"Yes." Mr. Renaldi walked up to the blackboard. "Now, 'The Metamorphosis' was written by Franz Kafka." He wrote the author's name on the board, then turned around. "What does it mean to call something Kafkaesque? Brian?"

"When something seems like a total nightmare. And you can't believe it's happening, only...it is," Brian said.

Angela stared at Sharon. She had never seen somebody actually *glow* before.

"Can you give me an example of something Kafkaesque?" Mr. Renaldi asked the class.

Sharon Cherski having a boyfriend. And not me.

Sharon having this great body. And me having a zit.

Sharon making out with Kyle, like, in the flesh. And me only making out with Jordan on a piece of paper, in a rumor, in a note.

She couldn't *stop* giving examples of things that were Kafkaesque.

Angela stepped closer to the new poster in the girls' room. On it was the new model she kept seeing everywhere, like on every single magazine, in every perfume, cosmetics, and clothing ad she'd seen in the past week. IT'S NOT COOL TO SMOKE IN SCHOOL was printed at the bottom.

As if someone who looks like that ever has to worry about what people think of her. Whether she's cool or not is so not the point. She doesn't have to care, because she's, like...above the standards people use.

Rickie threw up his hands. "It has nothing to do with what anyone said. I just always knew why I was coming in here, okay? But if people are going to take it wrong, or give it this meaning that I don't even want it to have—"

"Ashley DiMarco asked me if you were getting a sex change," Rayanne said.

"Exactly!" Rickie cried. "I don't want to be a girl. I want to *hang* with girls. There's a huge difference. But if other people can't understand, then it's good-bye, empty soap dispensers! Good-bye, dripping, scummy faucets! Good-bye, too-hot radiator that I was always burning my butt on!" Rickie blew a kiss at the radiator. "Oh, Scarecrow, I think I'll miss you most of all!" He grabbed Angela's arms and danced her around the bathroom while they both laughed.

Suddenly the door swung open and somebody tossed a piece of paper into the room, then took off down the hallway. Rayanne darted to the door.

"Who was that? What is it?" Angela asked.

"He got away," Rayanne said, gazing down the hallway. She picked up the sheet of yellow paper. "Oh my God—you will not believe this. Sophomore girls: The Top Forty!"

"What?" Angela cried.

"Okay, the first one is obvious. Hottest sophomore babe—"

"Casey Hall," Angela and Rickie chimed in.

"Best butt, Leslie Godfrey. Well, that's true. She's in front of me in homeroom." Rayanne flipped her hair over her shoulder. "Best legs, Jennifer Kaminsky. Excuse me? In what universe!"

"Have you seen her ankles?" Rickie made a face as he peered over Rayanne's shoulder at the list.

"Wait—Sharon Cherski?" Angela cried.

"Who?" Rickie asked. "Oh, your ex-best…"

"They *are* quite sizable," Rayanne commented.

"Things like this make me sick," Angela muttered. "It's so stupid, I mean, who asked them? What gives them the right to—"

"Angela! Look!" Rayanne shrieked. "I'm on it!"

"What?"

"Look—most slut potential!" Rayanne threw the list into the air. "Do you love it or what?"

Rickie picked up the poll and scanned it. "Don't worry, Angela. You're not on it."

"I don't *care*!" Angela cried. "If I'm on it or not. That's not the point. It's still incredibly stupid."

"I just meant, you're lucky. You don't get noticed; you blend in." He shrugged and shoved the list into the trash can. "Unlike me. Who basically doesn't fit in anywhere and never will."

Lucky…

The worst feeling is suddenly realizing that you don't measure up. And that, in the past, when you thought you did? You were a fool.

Angela stared at her face in the mirror, and all she could see was this lump on her chin, and she imagined it growing bigger and bigger, until she didn't have a face left at all.

Later that day Angela sat on the couch, waiting for dinner to be ready, ignoring her mother. Patty kept trying to convince her to be in the same mother-daughter fashion show for charity they'd done last year with Sharon Cherski and *her* mother. Wasn't it obvious that Angela was too old for things like that? Not her mother, although maybe it was borderline. But Angela wasn't about to be seen wearing an outfit that matched anybody's, least of all her mother's.

Never mind the fashion show—or the fact that she and Sharon had modeled together the year before and now they were barely speaking. She was supposed to be studying; she was supposed to be writing a paper about "The Metamorphosis."

She turned to a fresh page in the back of her notebook and wrote in capital letters:

ANGELA CHASE, THE DIARY OF A YOUNG DIDN'T-MAKE-THE-TOP-40 GIRL

Lists, notes, and gossip, she thought. *Is this what everything boils down to after a certain point? Like whatever we are, if we can even figure that out, doesn't matter. The only thing that matters is who and what other people think we are, and how they rank us.*

But I refuse to believe that. Despite the evidence to the contrary. Because if that's true, and I'm not on this list? That means I don't even exist. Even if it does feel that way sometimes, it's definitely not true all the time. For instance, this zit on my face proves I'm here. Clogged pores and all.

And does anyone ever really figure out what they want to look like? My mom cut her hair very short recently, like it was some big change in her life, like it would change everything. Some metamorphosis. She's still Mom, but with short hair.

And now she's getting all obsessed about aging, which is totally depressing. Because if she's worrying about getting older, and I'm worrying about not being old enough, that means there's, like, this incredibly short period in our lives when we're actually happy with the age we are. Like, when we're twenty or twenty-two, maybe.

"Angela!" her mother called out from the kitchen. "Are you sure you don't want to do the fashion show?"

Two more days had passed, and it was still there. *It can't get any bigger. It cannot. It is medically impossible.* Angela was starting to think that her face was auditioning for a part in a pimple medication ad. She had run into the girls' bathroom to check and see if it had disappeared, by some miracle, as if she couldn't still feel that it was there, every single second. *How self-conscious can a person get before they, like, turn inside out?*

She was leaning up to the mirror, examining her chin, when Sharon walked into the girls' room. Without saying a word, Sharon took a brush out of her leather purse, shook her hair out of its barrette, and started fixing her hair.

"Um...so are you doing that fashion show or whatever?" Angela asked. "Because my mom said you were. But I just wondered..." She paused, waiting for Sharon to acknowledge her. But Sharon kept brushing her hair, like Angela wasn't even standing two feet away from her. "So that's how it is now? I can't even ask you a *question*?"

Frustrated, Angela turned to leave. "Well, excuse me for daring to speak to you."

"Well, excuse me, but just because you suddenly decide I'm worth talking to, after ignoring me for, like, weeks—"

"I changed my mind. You're not worth talking to, okay?"

"Oh, go squeeze your zit," Sharon shot back.

Angela felt her stomach tighten with a sick, inferior feeling. How could Sharon say something like that? "Well, congratulations." The words fired out of her mouth before she could think about it. "About the poll. You must be *so* proud."

Sharon stopped brushing her hair. "Poll?"

"You didn't know? You're on it," Angela said, unable to hide the emotion in her voice, unable to resist the temptation to hurt back. "Actually, they both are. I can't believe you didn't know. I bet Kyle did."

Sharon stared at her, looking the same way Angela had felt a few seconds ago. Like the bottom had fallen out of something. Like they couldn't sink any lower. Angela felt guilty for a second. Then she turned around and walked out the door, leaving Sharon standing there, her hair half-styled and her face bright red.

Angela headed down the hallway, feeling slightly victorious. Maybe she did have a zit, but she still had a voice. She could still stand up for herself. *It's one dumb list, not the absolute truth.*

Then she rounded the corner and saw Jordan leaning against a locker, deep in conversation with Casey Hall. *Of course he's with sophomore girl number one. Not sophomore girl zero.*

When Jordan looked up and saw her, Angela put her

hand over her chin. Casey smiled at her, the bright whiteness of her teeth practically casting a beam of light in the dusky, dim hallway. *Is this cosmic payback or something, for what I just said to Sharon?*

"Hi," Angela said, only it came out more like a hoarse croak. *Great. Now I've turned into a frog. Kafka's little-known sequel: Metamorphosis II.*

"Look, stop screwing around, just pop it. Okay? So you can get on with your life," Rayanne urged the next day at Angela's house. She, Rickie, and Angela were crowded around the small mirror on Angela's dresser.

"Won't I get a scar?" Angela asked.

"Anything causes a scar. Living causes a scar," Rayanne said. "My mother has a major scar from when she had me. Does that mean I should never have been born?"

Angela didn't want to think about childbirth. She was having enough trouble with one little—okay, maybe *not* so little—pimple. "So...you guys think I should pop it?"

Rayanne sighed loudly. "I have to go."

"I'll go with you," Rickie said. "Just *don't* put concealer on it, because it'll make things even worse."

Once Rickie and Rayanne had left, Angela just stood in front of her dresser, looking into the mirror. *Go away. Please.*

Her mother knocked lightly on the open door and came into her room, carrying two identical dresses. "I'm almost finished, and I wanted to check the fit on you." She held a dress out to Angela.

"Mom..." Angela didn't take the hanger from her.

"Don't you want to try it on?"

"Mom…I don't want to *be* in that fashion show. I can't tell you again, because I'm repeating myself constantly," Angela said.

"Well, I don't understand why you don't want to be in it. I would think you'd welcome the opportunity to dress up and look your best," her mother said.

"Mom, who am I supposed to look my best for? You or me?"

"For you, of course it's for you. I don't care about—"

"Mom, look, just face the facts, okay?" Angela said, finally turning away from the mirror.

"What facts? What are you talking about?"

"That I'm *ugly*, okay? Just face it. *I* have," Angela said.

"How can you say that? How can you possibly—"

Angela threw down the Q-Tip she'd been clenching. It bounced off the dresser onto the floor. "By looking in the mirror, okay? And by looking at you, and the way you look at me."

"How do I look at you?" her mother asked, appearing confused.

"And how you tell me how to wash my face constantly so I won't get zits, like you have to fix me, like you're ashamed—"

"No, Angela! I never said that! I never meant—"

"Because you want me to be as beautiful as *you*. Well, sorry, I'm not. I'm just *not*!" Angela pushed back her chair and walked out of the room.

Angela stood in front of the mirror in the girls' bathroom at school the next morning, carefully applying a fresh coat of Ivory Beige with a cover-up stick. *Ivory Beige. Isn't that, like, a contradiction in terms? It sounds like a color for dead people*.

One of the stall doors behind her opened. In the mirror, Angela saw Sharon. She capped the cover on the stick, tossed it into her backpack, and opened another compartment, pretending to search for something else. Sometimes she wondered how she'd ever make it through the day without her backpack. It was so good to hide behind, like nylon armor.

"So. Look," Sharon said. "Are you doing this fashion show thing or not? Because my mom keeps saying you are, like, as a way to make me do it."

"I was going to do it? But I'm not," Angela said. She looked up at Sharon. "Are you?"

"No. But my mom still thinks we are. She's having this problem with denial." Sharon smiled. Angela noticed that one side of her mouth still curled up more than the other, the way it had ever since she was a little kid.

"Same with my mom," Angela said, nodding.

Sharon walked over to the poster on the wall, the one with the gorgeous model that said IT'S NOT COOL TO SMOKE IN SCHOOL. Now that it had been up for a few days, it was covered with graffiti. The model's face had black marks drawn on it, a mustache. The word PIG was scrawled across her chest.

"Why do girls have to tear each other down?" Sharon asked, staring at the poster.

Angela shrugged. "I guess because they're…jealous." She glanced down at a crumpled piece of brown paper on the floor. "I mean, I guess…maybe I said those things the other day because I was. Of you. For having…you know. What you have."

Sharon looked at Angela as if she had just told her the dispensers were full of soap. "Do you know how many times this week I wished I could have what *you* have?"

"I don't have anything!" Angela scoffed.

"Exactly," Sharon said.

Angela opened her mouth, about to protest, about to tell Sharon, "You're not supposed to say that, you're supposed to say, 'Of course you do!'" when she realized that Sharon was right. She didn't have anything. And it was so sad, it was almost funny. She smiled. "Well, this really makes sense."

"I guess it all boils down to what they used to drill into us at Girl Scouts," Sharon said.

"Sell more cookies or you can forget about that badge?" Angela asked.

"No! You know. What you are, like, what your gift is...wait, that's not it." Sharon looked confused.

"Wait—I've got it," Angela said excitedly. "What you *have* is God's gift—"

"—to you, and what you—"

"—do with what you have, is your gift—"

"—to God," they said together.

"Exactly." Sharon grinned.

"I can't believe you, like, *remember* that," Angela said.

"And you didn't?" Sharon teased.

And Angela knew all of a sudden that even though she and Sharon weren't ever going to be the same, together, again, that it would be okay. That maybe they'd find some other way to be friends. Not in the same every-day, I'll-do-whatever-you-do way. But in another, quieter way.

"Anyway," Sharon continued, "that little phrase has been drilled into me since birth, like mind control. My mom still has Girl Scout cookies from three *years* ago in the freezer."

Angela cracked up laughing. "Really? What flavor?"

"Thin mint, of course," Sharon said.

"Aren't they, like, thin *ice* by now?" Angela asked.

Suddenly the door opened, and Rayanne strode into the girls' room, walking right between the two of them. Angela took a step away from Sharon, who was already beginning to head for the door.

"So, hi, where've you been?" Angela asked Rayanne as Sharon went out into the hallway.

"What was she doing, bragging about her and Kyle's sex life?" Rayanne asked.

"No," Angela said.

"Look, if you want to be friends with her again, it's fine with me," Rayanne snapped.

"I don't!" Angela cried.

"Maybe you do. After all, she's not a slut, at least not yet," Rayanne said. "I know that me being picked for most slut potential has totally been bugging you."

"It hasn't," Angela insisted. "My bad mood lately has nothing to do with what was written about *you* on the list."

"Wait. I think I'm insulted," Rayanne said.

"No! Look, how many people you do or don't sleep with is, like, *so* not my business. It has nothing to do with our friendship. Okay?"

Rayanne nodded, considering it. "Okay. So what were you thinking about then?"

Angela just stared at her. "We're talking high altitude here. And it's not going away."

"Oh. That. Well, no offense? But you need a lot more cover-up to hide a zit that big." She started rummaging around in her huge shoulder bag. "What color are you using, anyway?"

"Ivory Beige," Angela said.

"Well, there you go, there's the whole problem," Rayanne declared. "What you need? Is something basic, like...Fair."

Fair, Angela thought, glancing at the defaced poster again and remembering what Sharon had said. *As if fairness had anything to do with anything.*

"She's pretty, isn't she?"

"They all are."

Angela smiled as a teenage girl came down the runway that Saturday night, followed by the girl's mother. Both wore matching sweaters and skirts. Angela was standing in the back of the room between Rayanne and Rickie, watching the walkway and waiting for her mother and Danielle.

She had never thought she'd be caught dead at another mother-daughter fashion show. But Rickie had refashioned her dress to fit Danielle, who'd confessed that she'd always wanted to be in the show. And here Angela was, watching pair after pair of mothers and daughters, and waiting for Patty and Danielle. The amazing thing was, to Angela, how great everyone looked— just because they were so obviously happy and were doing something together. No matter what size, shape, color, or skin type they were.

Sometimes it seems like we're all living in some kind of prison. And the crime is how much we hate ourselves.

Sharon Cherski and her mother, Camille, came down the runway next. Sharon looked slightly uncomfortable at first, but when they stepped into the spotlight, she smiled, looking around the audience. When she saw Angela, her face lit up even more.

It's good to get really dressed up once in a while, thought Angela. *And admit the truth—*

"Oh, look—Rickie!" Angela cried as Danielle stepped out of the wings. Beside her, Angela's mother walked confidently, proudly even. Watching the two of them together, Angela could see herself, all those years, tagging alongside in her mother's latest creation.

—that when you really look closely? People are so strange and so complicated that they're actually...beautiful.

Angela waved to her mother.

Possibly even me.

Chapter 6

"I thought you said you would never again hang in the girls' room," Rayanne said on Monday morning.

Rickie leaned close to the mirror and smudged the charcoal eyeliner under his eye into a softer line. "Never say never."

Kind of the way I feel about drinking, Rayanne thought, slyly taking a swig from the half-pint bottle of vodka in her bag. She stuffed it back into an inside pocket. She'd tried days at school without drinking—but they always seemed so much...longer.

The door opened and Sharon Cherski walked in. She gave Rickie a strange look. In Rayanne's opinion, Sharon was the kind of person who couldn't handle androgyny. In Sharon's universe, boys went to the boys' room, girls to the girls'. Nobody ever *crossed over*.

"Hi! What's wrong with your hair?" Rayanne asked. Sharon looked like she had just walked through a wind tunnel.

"Just…never mind," Sharon replied. She took a brush out of her purse, fiddled with a few out-of-place strands of hair, then frowned at her reflection in the mirror.

"You need some *mousse* or something?" Rayanne suggested. "'Cause that's what girls like you use, right? Mousse? The kind that smells like apples. Wait, wait! I've got something." Rayanne suddenly remembered that she had some kind of hair product in her bag, and started searching through it. The money her deadbeat father had recently sent her for her birthday—four months late—was stuffed into the bag, and the deeper she dug, the more money started falling out onto the floor. She kept trying to be careful, but she couldn't seem to control her hands. It was like the money had static cling.

"Rayanne! You're dropping all your money!" Rickie said.

"I don't care," Rayanne said. She held up a fistful of tens. "It's so crispy. Like dead leaves." *God, I can be profound*.

"How much have you had to drink today?" Rickie asked.

"She's been *drinking*?" Sharon sounded horrified.

I am shocked and appalled, Rayanne thought with a giggle. Sharon reminded her of Ms. Jenkins, her sixth-grade teacher, who had been shocked and appalled by Rayanne so often that she'd retired a year later. "There is no drinking in school, don't you know that?" Rayanne shook her finger in Sharon's face. She held out the money to Sharon. "Here, you don't like your hair? Buy yourself a wig."

"Stop it," Rickie said, grabbing Rayanne's arm.

Sharon stuffed her brush into her purse and, after one last glance at Rayanne, headed out the door.

"Don't go! Don't go!" Rayanne called after her. She turned to Rickie. "Here, you take it, I want you to have it—"

"Don't be crazy," Rickie said.

"I'm serious—you deserve it more than me," Rayanne said.

"Rayanne." Rickie started stuffing the money he'd picked up from the floor back into her bag. "You should buy something for yourself. I mean, think—what do you really need? New makeup, new CDs, a leather jacket—"

What I really need. "Rickie, you are so brilliant. A party!"

Rickie stopped picking up the money and looked at her.

"Like an event. Like a memory I'll have for the rest of my life," Rayanne said. "Where there's so much going on at every second that there's no possibility for your mind to wander." *And for you to start thinking about things, like the fact that your dad just sent you two hundred and seventy dollars just to make up for being an absolute low-life. As a bribe, possibly.* "Yes. A party."

Angela was walking down the hallway Friday afternoon when Rayanne ran straight at her, almost tackling her. "Angela! Some girl just invited me—to my own house! The word of mouth is, like, huge on this thing," Rayanne said. "Saturday is going to be *historical*."

"Wait." Angela hesitated. "This Saturday?"

"Yes, this Saturday! Tomorrow night!" Rayanne said. She gave Angela a doubtful look. "I mentioned this at least a dozen times."

"But tomorrow night is that thing for my grandparents," Angela said. "That wedding anniversary party.

Like, the golden one or whatever."

Rayanne raised one eyebrow. "Fine. Go hang with your grandparents. You can sit around eating soft foods all night." She turned and started walking away.

Angela felt terrible. Everyone she knew would be at Rayanne's, she was going to miss the biggest party of the year, and it obviously meant a lot to Rayanne that she wasn't coming.

"Hey, Angela," Rayanne said, turning around. "I'm a bitch. I know."

Angela shrugged. She walked up to Rayanne. "If I can't come, maybe I could...I don't know. Help you get ready."

"Help? How?" Rayanne asked.

"I don't know. I always put up streamers at our house," Angela said.

"Streamers?" Rayanne said. "What exactly is a streamer, anyway? How does that have anything to do with a stream?"

"So...can I help?" Angela asked.

On Friday night, Angela walked into her house and closed the front door quietly behind her. She'd spent the evening with Rayanne and her mother, Amber, eating pizza, reading tarot cards, and getting their apartment ready for Rayanne's party on Saturday. When she walked into the dining room, she saw her mother standing on a chair, hanging streamers.

Angela smiled. "Mom, I said I would do it."

"Well, I'm doing it," her mother replied in an irritated voice.

"Just leave it. I'll do them in the morning," Angela offered. She hated when her mother got stressed and cranky. She was absolutely impossible to deal with...for hours.

"There are a million *other* things to do in the morning."

"Oh. All right. I didn't realize it was that big of a deal." Angela ran her finger along the dusty edge of the bookcase. "Mom, so it turns out...there's this birthday party at Rayanne's. And it's sort of tomorrow. That's why I got home so late, I was there helping," she explained.

"You were helping with *Rayanne's* party?"

"Mom. Could I maybe spend some time here tomorrow night, and then go to Rayanne's?"

"Forget it!" her mother cried. "I need you here. This is a very big deal, having a large party like this at our house, and—"

"You're only having it here instead of at a restaurant because Grandma talked you into it!" Angela cried.

"That's not true," her mother said.

Angela sighed. "You know, Amber was telling me about karma tonight—"

"Amber? You call her Amber?"

"And the karma in this house is, like, ridiculous right now," Angela continued.

"Really," her mother sneered.

"Yes. It's really bad...or dark. Or whatever happens to karma."

"And I suppose the karma at *Amber's* is through the roof, right? Listen to me, Angela. You are not going to Rayanne's tomorrow. You are going to be here, for your grandparents' anniversary. Is that clear?"

Angela just stared at her mother. The scale couldn't even measure karma that low. It was like...basement karma. Cold, damp, and poorly lit.

Rickie stood under a red lightbulb, glancing as unobtrusively as possible at a guy who'd just walked into Rayanne's apartment. He'd never seen the guy before. He was cute.

The guy disappeared into the kitchen, and Rickie was left smiling politely at the hordes of people filing into Rayanne's. He sipped from his can of orange soda and looked around the living room. *I wish somebody would show up that I know. Because the point of a party is to, like...talk to people. Isn't it?*

Rayanne passed in front of him in a flash. Rickie glimpsed a small bag in her hand. "Rayanne!" he called, yelling to be heard over the blasting music. He followed her, dodging around people he didn't recognize.

Rayanne was just about to shut the bathroom door in his face when Rickie walked in. "Rickie!" she cried. "Come on in. Is this satanic or what?"

"Who *are* all these people?" Rickie asked.

"I have no idea!" Rayanne said happily. "There's faces here I've never seen. There's people I don't think are from Pennsylvania. Hey, have you seen Tino?" Rayanne fished two pills out of the plastic bag in her hand.

"Rayanne, I'm lucky I found *you*," Rickie said. He stared at the pills. "What are you doing?"

Rayanne popped the two pills into her mouth. She washed them down with a gulp of beer.

"Rayanne!" Rickie couldn't stand it when Rayanne took drugs. Or drank. Or did both. Which was way too often lately.

"What?" Rayanne said, shaking her head at him, her braids swirling around her face. "It's only two little pills."

Rickie couldn't watch. He turned to open the door

and go back to the party.

"Boy Scout!" Rayanne called after him.

I want to protect Rayanne so much that sometimes it actually hurts. Like a physical pain in my side. It's like... if I feel the pain myself, then maybe I can stop her from hurting herself.

Only it doesn't work.

"Hi, Grandma, happy anniversary," Angela said, walking into the kitchen. She gave her grandmother a big hug. *What's horrible is when your parents get their way, and it's over something that seems so utterly meaningless. Only it means a lot.* Angela smiled as brightly as she could. "Where's Grandpa?"

"Tell her," Angela's mother said.

"I have to check the turkey." Her grandmother leaned over the oven.

"You want to know where Grandpa is? He's not coming," Patty informed Angela.

"You mean...he's back in the hospital?" Angela asked.

Her mother shook her head. "No."

"Oh," said Angela. "You mean he's just not coming?"

"Well...yes."

"So Grandpa's not even coming, but *I* have to be here? That makes sense!"

"You don't have to be here." Angela's grandmother turned around, holding a basting bulb. "If you've got better plans—"

Patty shook her head. "Doesn't anyone care about *family?* How about doing what's right?"

"What's right? What's *right?*" Angela argued. "I can't believe it! We're having a party for someone who isn't here. And I'm missing Rayanne's party."

"Who's Rayanne?" her grandmother asked.

"My best friend," Angela said.

"You're missing your best friend's party?"

"Rayanne isn't her best friend," Patty insisted.

"Mom! She is so my best friend! I'm sorry you hate her!" Angela cried. "But I'd much rather be—"

"Oh, *yes*," her mother said. "You'd much rather be over at Rayanne's, where you can all guzzle beer, and Amber can read your tea leaves—"

"Tarot cards. And Rickie and I don't drink," Angela informed her, just before she headed out the back door.

"Angela! To see you. At this moment. I mean, something was…you know, missing. Then I turn around and—I just love you so much!" Rayanne pulled Angela into a hug, her bottle of cold beer pressing against Angela's back, leaving a wet mark.

"Yeah, it's great! Wow!" Angela said, struggling to hold up Rayanne, who was listing to one side. *She's already drunk*, Angela realized. *And I just got here. There's a weird feeling when someone you're close to is…gone. Behind this wall of, like, alcohol.*

Angela let go of Rayanne for a second, and Rayanne fell to the floor, howling with laughter. Rickie appeared and helped her to her feet.

"Hey, Rickie! My two best friends…Rickie and Angela. Rickie," Rayanne giggled. "Show Angela where all the cute boys are."

"Rayanne. Give me your beer, okay?" Rickie said, reaching for the bottle.

"Oh my God! There are people here who have *graduated*. There is a guy here doing *tattoos*," Rayanne said.

"Hey! Can you do one like this?" She picked a tarot card off the floor and stumbled across the living room.

That's the Death card, Angela realized. "Rickie…"

"I've been through this before," Rickie said quickly. "She'll be okay. She always—"

"What the—hey!" The music abruptly ended, and Angela saw Rayanne's mother standing by the stereo, looking horrified. "Okay, party's over, everyone. Out! Rayanne, I want everyone out of here in two minutes or I'm calling the cops!"

Having your mother shut down your party is one of the worst things that can happen. Not that I've ever had a party.

People started scrambling toward the door, pulling themselves up off the floor or the couch, dropping beer cans on the kitchen table, sorting through a giant pile of coats by the door. When everyone was finally out the door, Amber turned to Rayanne.

"You said you were going to have a few friends over. Look at this! This place is a pig sty! I've got five minutes before I gotta meet Rusty, and this house is destroyed!" Amber started sorting through her purse, angrily tossing items onto the dresser in her bedroom.

"Sorry." Rayanne was walking into the bedroom when she stumbled and fell.

Angela started to move toward her, but Rickie held her arm.

"No, *I'm* sorry," Amber said. "Look at you! You are too drunk, young lady. Way too drunk. What did I say about moderation? I trusted you!"

Rayanne slowly crawled from the floor up onto the bed. Angela watched her, wondering why Amber wasn't helping her daughter.

"Look at you. Like an old drunk," Amber said, sounding completely disgusted. She put the cap on her lipstick. "Pull yourself together. I want this whole place cleaned up by the time I get back."

Amber put a few finishing touches on her makeup and then went out of the house, slamming the door behind her.

Angela stared at Rayanne, who was practically passed out on the bed. Rickie was crouched beside her, pulling her leg out from where it had twisted underneath her. Angela couldn't get over the fact that Amber had just left, as if what was happening didn't concern her at all. As if a date was more important than Rayanne.

"Rickie, I love you. You know that? But...I'm so *cold*." Rayanne's eyes began to close, and her body shivered once.

"Okay, just take it easy," Rickie said.

"Oh my God, Rickie—what's happening to her?" Angela asked.

"She's going to be okay. I've done this before, okay, so don't worry," Rickie said confidently. "Let's get her into the bathroom."

Angela helped him lift Rayanne off the bed. They each wrapped one of her arms around their shoulder. Angela had never felt such a limp body before. Rayanne's skin was damp, and cold. "Gonna have to...sleep a little while," Rayanne said as they set her down on the tile floor.

"Get water," Rickie ordered Angela.

She quickly filled a cup next to the sink and started to hand it to Rickie. "Throw it on her face!" he shouted.

Angela splashed the cupful on Rayanne, but she didn't respond.

"Rayanne! You can't go to sleep! Wake up!" Rickie cried.

All the information Angela had learned at school about drinking and taking drugs was flashing through her brain in a jumble of mismatched facts. Everyone always said you had to keep somebody awake—but how did you actually *do* that when they were slipping away right in front of you? "Rickie?"

"I've never seen her this bad. Oh God, I don't know what to do!" Rickie finally admitted. "Angela?"

Angela stared at Rayanne's pale face, at the way her hands were lying palm up, her wrists at unnatural angles. "I know what to do," she said. She rushed to the telephone.

Angela's mother walked through the door, and Angela threw her arms around her, clinging for a second longer than she usually did.

Patty smoothed her hair. "I called an ambulance. They'll be here any minute. Where is she?"

Angela led her mother back through the apartment and into the bathroom. Patty kneeled beside Rayanne. She slapped Rayanne's face and turned to Rickie. "How long has she been this way?"

"You mean...how long..."

"This slow breathing," Patty said.

"A while. Fifteen minutes, maybe?" Rickie said.

"What did she take?"

"She had a lot to drink," Rickie said. "And..."

"What *drugs*?" Patty said, shaking Rayanne awake. "Names. I need names."

"Well, I know she took some Ecstasy, because—"

"How much?"

"I wasn't watching, but I think...two hits, probably. She had this little plastic bag, and I *told* her—" Rickie started to cry, and Angela touched his shoulder.

"Find me the bag. Find out if there are some left. And get me a blanket." Rickie jumped up and ran into the bedroom. He came back carrying a blanket, and Patty started wrapping it around Rayanne, just as they heard a knock at the door. "That's the ambulance."

Angela thought of the night they'd gone to Let's Bolt, when Rickie told her Rayanne wouldn't remember what happened because she blacked out. And she thought of what Rayanne had said in the police car afterward, how she'd promised to look out for Angela. "I'll always watch out for you. I'll always be there for you. So don't worry."

Angela felt numb as she watched the paramedics come into the bathroom and start strapping Rayanne onto a stretcher. As if she were watching the whole thing from very far away. As if she were watching somebody else almost lose her best friend.

"God. I still can't believe she had to have her *stomach* pumped," Rickie said as Angela's mother parked the car in the Chase driveway about an hour later. They'd invited Rickie back to their house when they left the hospital, after Amber showed up to take care of Rayanne.

Angela was trying not to think about it. She smiled wanly at Rickie.

"Could you go in and tell everyone we'll be there in a minute?" her mother asked.

Rickie nodded and opened the door, getting out of the car.

Angela slid over on the seat into the space Rickie had

left. "I guess I sort of screwed up everything for you tonight. You missed the party," she said.

"No. You did the right thing. You called me." Patty paused. "Promise me you'll always do that, that you'll always—"

"Okay!" Angela said. "Okay, I will." She stared at her mother. "So how did you know how to do those things tonight?"

"What? Oh. Well, I had a roommate in college. Who was actually a lot like Rayanne," her mother confessed.

"You're kidding." *My mother used to hang out with cool people?* "So what happened?"

"Well, pretty much what happened tonight," her mother said slowly. "Except...she died."

Angela stared at her mother. She didn't know what to say. All she could think about was the way Rayanne had been lying on the cold bathroom floor, half-dead, her long hair fanned out around the bottom of the sink. "So...she was your friend?" Angela asked. "You liked her?"

"A lot. Angela, I don't know what to do. But your future is starting to scare me. And I don't know if I should just not let you *see* her anymore or—"

"No. Mom! I can't do that. She's my *friend*." Angela put her hand on her mother's arm. "Trust me."

"Actually, I do." Patty turned to Angela and hugged her.

"Oh God!" Angela said. "Poor Rickie, he's stuck in there, surrounded by our relatives." She laughed.

But suddenly, that didn't seem like such a bad place to be.

Chapter 7

"God, he's so *flat*." Angela was lying on her bed, staring at the ceiling. Danielle was lying beside her. The sound of a slightly off-key saxophone was wafting through the open window on the brisk air of late October.

It was Sunday night. A week had passed since Rayanne's party, and things had gotten back to normal. Rayanne had agreed to see a school counselor regularly and to stay away from drinking, drugs, and partying in general. And so far, she had.

A squeaky high note suddenly hit Angela's ear—or more like assaulted it. "It's no wonder the whole neighborhood is awake."

"Don't you think he's...kind of cool, though?" Danielle asked.

"Brian? Krakow?" Angela almost pushed Danielle off the bed.

"Well, sometimes he says really cool things—"

"Oh my God, you have a *crush* on Brian Krakow," Angela said.

"Do not," Danielle replied calmly.

"Don't get all weird and defensive. I used to have lots of crushes when I was young." *Like, last year. Or was that September?* "They're totally normal."

"So what's the difference between...you know, a crush and being in love?" Danielle asked.

"First of all, you are *not* in love with Brian Krakow, so don't even tell me that. But the difference? Okay. Love is...when you look into someone's eyes? And you don't just see their face. You go, like, all the way into their soul. And you both know, instantly."

Danielle gazed at Angela. "Wow. And this can happen, like, anywhere? I mean, at the supermarket or the post office or—"

"Not really," Angela explained. "It usually only happens when you're doing something more interesting. Like you're traveling by yourself on an airplane and someone starts talking to you. Or say you're in a big crowd. In Paris. And then suddenly—"

"I get it," Danielle said, yawning. "It's magical."

"Right," Angela said. "And it's *never* somebody like Brian. It's somebody else. Somebody you really don't know yet."

Beside her, Danielle had curled up into a ball. "Danielle, you are not sleeping here with me," Angela said. But she knew it was too late—her sister was already asleep. So she reached up and turned out the light on her night table. A few minutes later, the saxophone noise stopped. She punched her pillow and turned over a few times.

But half an hour later, she was still wide awake. She couldn't stop thinking about Jordan.

She kept replaying every conversation she'd had with Jordan, everything she said—which was painfully stupid—and everything he said—or didn't say. There were a lot of scenes that involved him leaning, or putting breath freshener in his mouth, or Visine in his eyes. He just never said very much.

There were so many things she'd always wanted to say to him but never had. Like:

You have the most amazing eyes.

Please give me that flannel shirt you always wear.

I think our souls are meant to be together.

What kind of breath freshener is that? (She'd gotten close enough to know that it really worked.)

You're so beautiful, it hurts to look at you.

She started having an imaginary conversation with Jordan, wondering what he'd say to her. Maybe he had questions that he'd always wanted to ask her.

Are you really from France? (Rayanne had told Jordan that to convince him that Angela couldn't ask him to make her a fake I.D. because she hadn't quite mastered the language.)

Why do you always stare at me like that, like you can see into my soul?

Do you ever let go of your backpack?

You're so beautiful, it hurts to look at you.

Angela couldn't lie there anymore, pretending to sleep. Her mind was racing. She quietly pulled back the covers, got up, and crept over to her dresser, where she'd left her notebook. Then, grabbing a pen from the red plastic cup on her desk, she sat on the floor, in a pool of moonlight, and leaned back against her bed.

"Dear Jordan," she wrote.

"People! Don't forget to stay with the group!"

Rayanne stared into a diorama called *The Theory of Evolution*. "Do you think that's how it really happened?"

Rickie shrugged. "Who knows? I mean, half of the stuff in this place could be made up. It's not like people were around to make sure."

"What are you saying? This is natural history," Angela argued. "There are, like, observations and facts and everything to back all this stuff up."

Rayanne sighed. "God, she's so innocent."

Angela hit Rayanne's arm. "Shut up!"

"The most important thing to remember is to stay with the group!" Ms. Cligman, their chaperon for the day, cried out into the Fossils Room.

"*What* is the big deal about staying with the group?" Angela asked. "What if Amelia Earhart had stayed with the group?"

"Or Diana Ross?" Rickie suggested.

"Or Perry Farrell...or Sting!" Rayanne added, checking out a male museum guard who was standing over in the corner.

"Hey, Rayanne. I have to show you something," Angela whispered.

"Oh yeah? What?" Rayanne kept staring at the guard. When he looked in her direction, she smiled. "I'd like him to show me something," she said under her breath.

Angela pulled the folded-up five-page letter out of her backpack. She'd reread it so many times that morning, she almost had it memorized. "Last night, I couldn't sleep? So I wrote this. It contains everything I have ever wanted to express to Jordan Catalano."

"You're going to send this to him?" Rayanne looked horrified.

"No! It's…private. I just wanted to show it to you, because I'm proud of it. I mean, I think I'm finally *over* him."

"'Dear Jordan,'" Rayanne read softly "'It is now twelve forty-five A.M. and…'" She shifted through the pages. "So, like, what did you say?"

"Just, you know, everything. Like I admit how I was, you know, overpoweringly attracted to him or whatever, but I point out how he could have handled things differently? And that he never really knew me or understood me…and how I was obsessed with him once, but how that's totally over now."

Rayanne glanced at the pages, then at Angela. "So can I read the whole thing?"

"Yeah, but…just you, okay? Don't show it to anyone," Angela said.

"I wouldn't!" Rayanne cried.

"People, we will now be moving to the Wall of Quadrupeds!" Ms. Cligman yelled.

"Hey, Chase. She said to stay with the *group*."

Angela turned around. "Go practice your scales, Krakow." For a second she thought about Danielle, and how she'd be thrilled right now if Brian were telling her to stay with the group. But Danielle would get over her crush on Brian, the same way she'd gotten over Jordan. Things were different between them now. She didn't even feel that nervous about the fact that Jordan was on the same field trip, that he had sat two seats behind her on the bus. That was all…history now. Unnatural history.

She walked around a corner, away from Brian, and

practically crashed into a huge reconstructed dinosaur skeleton. She caught her breath. On the other side of the dinosaur bones was Jordan. He looked up and smiled faintly at her. Angela studied the dinosaur's front leg. Jordan was humming a song that she didn't recognize but wanted to, just to have something to say to him.

Jordan moved around the tail end of the dinosaur and abruptly stopped humming. "I've been humming this tune for, like, hours."

"Oh." Angela nodded. "Like you can't get it out of your mind? Or something?" *If only there were a button somewhere, that I could push. To force me to stop talking around him so stupidly. Maybe Brian was right. Maybe I should have stayed with the group.*

Jordan sighed. "I just can't take dinosaurs seriously since that movie." He glanced at Angela. "It's like they're overexposed or something, you know?"

"That's really true." *That's the most brilliant observation I've ever heard him make.* "I mean, that's *so* true," Angela repeated.

Jordan walked over, a little closer. "I could use a cup of coffee right about now."

"You drink coffee?" Angela felt somehow impressed. She thought Mountain Dew would have been Jordan's beverage of choice. But that was just a commercial, right? She looked into his eyes. "With cream?"

"Black. With three or four sugars." Jordan cleared his throat and started to walk away, toward the museum snack bar, Angela guessed. As he walked, he started humming again.

"So, what's that song, anyway? That you keep humming," Angela asked.

Jordan stopped, turning halfway around. "Just this

song I'm writing. I'm in this band now, Frozen Embryos? With Tino? So, I'm writing this song. Anyway, you should hear us sometime."

He drinks coffee. He writes songs. Angela knew more about Jordan from the last five minutes than she'd ever known before. If this kept going, maybe...

"That's great," she told him. "I mean, I'd love to hear—"

"Angela! Angela! Angela!" Sounding like a fire alarm, Rayanne skidded into the room.

"Yeah, well, anyway." Jordan shrugged and headed off.

"Rayanne, you will not believe this!" Angela said in an excited whisper, trying desperately to control herself. "Jordan Catalano was, like—"

"Angela!" Rayanne cried. "I have to talk to you!"

"Just listen for a second. Jordan was, like, having an actual conversation with me just now, like on purpose—a really nice conversation, and—"

"That's great, Angela. No, really." Rayanne chewed at her thumbnail. "Just...don't hate me, okay?"

"Why would I—" Angela suddenly remembered handing Rayanne the letter. And she hadn't seen Rayanne or the letter since..."No. Rayanne? No. You didn't!"

"I'm sorry. Really sorry. But—"

"Did you *show* it to him? I'll kill you!"

"No!" Rayanne sounded insulted. "I'd never show it to him. Like on purpose. But I did kind of misplace it."

"You what?!"

"I'm really sorry. I'll find it for you, I swear." She looked shyly at Angela. "On the plus side? I've been hanging out with that really cute guard from the Fossils

Room?" She paused. "Not that that makes it okay, on any level."

"Rayanne. You lost my letter. Which means...somebody else could have found it. Somebody like Sharon or Brian or..." All of a sudden, a horrible, scary, possibly true thought came to her. *Or Jordan.* "Jordan was just being nice to me. Like, for the first time. Out of absolutely nowhere."

"Oh," Rayanne said, looking worried. "Oh," she said again. "Well, don't worry. It'll be fine."

Why did I ever write that dumb letter? Couldn't I have just had insomnia like normal people, without making a record of it? Why did I have to put it down on paper for, like, history's sake?

She felt as exposed as the dinosaur that she and Jordan had just been pretending to study. It was like her bones and ribs had suddenly been put on view. And her heart. *He was humming, and we talked about coffee, and the whole time, I didn't know it, but I was standing there, naked.*

"So, Chase. You still have my *Autobiography of Malcolm X*, right?"

Angela was so busy staring at Jordan's back that she barely heard Brian. She'd been staring at him all through English class, and now that it was finally over, she had to make her move. "Yeah, sure," she said in a distracted tone.

"So I need it back!" Brian said. "Okay?"

"Okay!" Angela said, exasperated. Why didn't Brian stop lending her things if he was going to get all stressed about getting them back? He'd been doing that since he was four. He would let her borrow a Magic Marker for like…twenty-four hours. And then get upset because his nice little box wasn't complete.

Jordan started heading for the door, and Angela followed him. She had to get this over with, fast. She'd been obsessing about the letter for what felt like weeks, even though it had only been a day. "Umm…" She waited for him to turn around. "Look. On the field trip yesterday?"

"Oh, I almost forgot. Here." He pulled a thick square of folded papers out of his jacket pocket and dropped it on a desk near the door. "I found it at the museum."

Angela felt her heart start to pound, as if somebody had put his foot on an accelerator connected to her bloodstream. So she was right. The worst *had* happened. "Look, when I wrote that? It was actually about somebody else. This guy who was my boyfriend last summer. And I just used your name because…it was about stuff that nobody else should know. Private things. Because, well, he's dead now." She took the letter from Jordan, her hand shaking. That had to be the most stupid story she'd ever come up with, for any reason.

Jordan was looking at her as if she hadn't said anything at all. "Look, I didn't read it."

"Oh, sure. Do you actually expect me to believe that?" Angela scoffed.

Jordan shrugged and took a step backward. "I don't care—"

"You find this hugely long letter, and it begins with 'Dear Jordan,' and you expect me to believe you didn't read it?!" Angela cried.

"I read parts of it. Okay?" Jordan blinked.

"Do you think I'm really stupid or something?"

Angela demanded. "You expect me to believe that you only *glanced* at it?"

"It didn't hold my interest, okay?"

Angela's heart drastically contracted, like it had just been pricked with a pin. She was so angry and so sad at the same time that she didn't even know how to phrase a sentence that could express anything of what she was feeling. "Oh, really? It didn't hold your *interest*. I'm so *sorry*. And why was that?"

"Never mind." Jordan started to leave the room.

Angela walked around and stood in front of him, blocking his way. "No, I'm really curious. What exactly was it that was so incredibly boring about my letter? I mean, just tell me! Was it too emotional? Too personal? Were there too many big words—"

"Shut up!" Jordan suddenly shouted at her. He turned away.

From the force of his answer, Angela knew that somehow, she had hit a nerve. Somehow, she had said exactly what the problem was. And she felt terrible. But at the same time, she also felt privileged. Because she knew Jordan better right at this moment than she ever had before. "Listen, I didn't mean to—"

"It's not just the big words. It's all the words." Jordan turned around and looked at Angela. "I never said that out loud to anyone before."

It's okay, Angela wanted to tell him. *I can help you.* But that would be too obvious. He probably wouldn't want her to say that, anyway.

"Yo, Catalano!" Jordan's friend Shane called from the hallway, through the open classroom door.

Jordan and Angela each took a few steps back, like

they'd been caught doing something wrong. *As if having a real conversation is, like, against the law. Because sometimes, that's how it feels.*

"I just talked to Tino. He can get us into that loft to practice tonight," Shane said.

Jordan scuffed his suede sneaker against the floor. "Cool."

"So..." Shane glanced at Angela. "We should tell the other Embryos."

"Right," Jordan said, starting to leave.

"So, your band's rehearsing tonight?" Angela pressed.

Jordan shrugged. "I guess so. Yeah."

Angela swung her backpack back and forth. "Maybe I'll get to hear that song you wrote sometime. I mean..."

"Sure. Yeah. We're, like, rehearsing at the loft Tino found."

"So, you mean...should I come by the loft, or...?" Angela paused. She'd never invited herself to anything before. But she felt like she had to do *some*thing.

"Well, you know. Sure. Whatever," Jordan said.

"Catalano, let's *go*," Shane urged.

Jordan left the classroom. Angela leaned against the wall, about to collapse. Something was really about to happen. Or had already.

Jordan had found her letter. He knew how she felt about him. And she knew he couldn't read.

"Wait, here's the best part!" Rayanne said. She turned to Rickie, who was sitting beside her on the bleachers outside school, overlooking the track. "He asked Angela to watch his band rehearse tonight. Which I have been wanting to do so bad. Actually, Rickie and I should go with you," she told Angela. "So you don't look too obvious or eager or anything."

"So what is this *thing* that happened between you guys?" Rickie asked.

"I can't really talk about it," Angela said. "But it involves that letter."

"I knew it!" Rayanne cried. "He found the letter, and it made him want you. Am I right?"

Angela smiled. "Kind of."

"Angela! Do you realize what this means?" Rayanne leaned back, tilting her face toward the sun and adjusting her oval shades.

"Of course," Angela said confidently, then paused a moment. "What does it mean?"

"This *thing* between you and Jordan Catalano is, like, happening. And who is the person without whom none of this would ever have transpired? Who is the genius who accidentally-on-purpose lost the stupid letter in the first place? And who should you be thanking for the rest of your adult life?"

"Thank you, Rayanne," Angela said in a whiny voice.

"Don't mention it." Rayanne lifted her shades and winked at Angela.

Lofts have to be incredibly cool. There's, like, a rule written somewhere, maybe in the housing code. They have to have chrome fifties chairs and old metal soft-drink machines, the kind where you pull out bottles.

Angela sat on a worn brown loveseat next to Rickie, wondering when Jordan was going to stop torturing her. The way he was just sitting there, strumming his guitar, as if she, Rickie, and Rayanne weren't there.

"Let's go," Rickie said. "They're totally ignoring us."

"Not yet," Angela argued.

"Well, I gotta make a call," said Rayanne, getting up.

"Can't they at least stop tuning their guitars and play something?" Rickie asked.

Huge events take place on this planet every day. Earthquakes. Hurricanes. Glaciers even move. So why can't he just look at me?

"Hey," Jordan called.

Angela looked over at him.

"So you want to hear that song I was telling you about?" Jordan moved his chair slightly, and the metal legs made a harsh, scraping sound against the floor.

Angela nodded.

Jordan started to play. Then his voice began to softly sing over the easy chords of the guitar. "I was going nowhere fast, I was living in the past...Life went by in a blur, then I found her...She's all I need..."

Oh my God, Angela thought. *A love song. About somebody else.*

"That's what I said," Jordan continued singing. "I call her...Red."

"Oh my God," Rickie whispered, touching Angela's hair. "Red. That's *you*."

Red. He actually has, like...a name for me.

"She's my shelter from the storm, she keeps me warm...She's a place to rest my head...I call her Red." Jordan looked up. "That's all I have so far." Then he started tuning his guitar again.

Angela hopped off the couch and practically dragged Rickie with her over to a corner of the loft by the door, where Rayanne had just finished using the telephone.

"Rickie! I can't believe it!" Angela whispered loudly.

"I know," Rickie replied. "And I have two things I

have to tell you. One, your hair is kind of dried out and you should let me hot-oil it. Two, I'm in love with him too."

"I knew it," Angela said.

"No, it's okay. You're definitely more right for him— Red."

"So, I'm going to take off now," Rayanne said. "You're going to stay, right?"

"I don't know," Angela said. The whole idea of talking to Jordan after that song was too overwhelming.

"You have to stay," Rickie argued. "After that? I mean, that's the whole point."

"Rickie's right. Okay, so bye! Bye!" Rayanne called over to Shane and Jordan. Rickie waved at both of them, and he and Rayanne ran out the door.

Angela just stood there, feeling very strange. Like she had just gotten an award or something, simply for showing up. But now what was she supposed to do, or say? *Thanks for writing that song about me. So, you're, like, obsessed with me, too?* And she kept thinking: *It's true. Rayanne was right. Changing your hair color? It could, like, change your whole life. Because nobody would ever write a song called "Dirty Blond," and if they did? It would be, like, a whole different thing. A limerick, maybe.*

"So, you want to hang around, or you want me to drive you home?" Jordan called over to her.

Angela cleared her throat. "Drive me home."

Chapter 8

Jordan parked his red convertible by the curb in front of Angela's house. She desperately feared that her parents were sitting around waiting for a moment like this. She could just picture them, crouched by their bedroom window, watching. It was an awkward enough moment to live through on your own, without spectators.

"I was just thinking," Angela said nervously, eager to have something to talk about. "Could you maybe have dyslexia?"

"That backwards thing?" Jordan asked.

Angela nodded. "Lots of people have it, you know. Like my Uncle Neil has it, and it makes reading really hard because—"

"Let's not talk about this, okay?" Jordan interrupted.

"—your mind reverses things," Angela continued. "It's actually a sign of high intelligence. Dyslexia. I mean, just because a person can't read—"

"Hey, I can read," Jordan said defensively. "Okay? Just not...that *well*."

"No. I know," Angela said, nodding.

They sat in silence for a minute or two. Angela was afraid she'd said the wrong thing. *But how can you not talk about something when you both know it's, like, the key...*

"You know those guys, up in the mountains?" Jordan suddenly asked.

Angela stared at him, confused. "What guys? Hermits, you mean?" Did Jordan plan on becoming a hermit after high school? Did he think hermits didn't have to read?

"No, those guys who make snow. Like at ski resorts and stuff." He shifted in his seat, leaning toward her. "Who make snow, like, as their job."

Angela watched as Jordan's face came closer to hers. "Yeah," she whispered, the seat squeaking underneath her.

"I would really like to do that." Jordan sighed.

"You mean, like, part-time? Or—"

He leaned forward, put his hand on her cheek, and kissed her.

Everything I have ever heard or imagined about kissing...was a lie. It's so much better than that. Your lips are, like...a part of this other person all of a sudden. And it's Jordan Catalano.

"Sorry," Jordan sighed.

"For...for what?" Angela asked.

"I interrupted you. Like last time," he said.

"No." *This wasn't like last time. Believe me.* "I mean, it's okay," Angela said, her fingers on the door handle.

Somehow she knew that the moment had to end right then, or it would be turned into another, weaker moment, one she might not want to remember. "So…good night."

"Right."

She stood on the curb, watching as the red taillights on his car gradually faded into the misty night. She slowly walked across the lawn in front of her house. Then she started skipping, waving her arms in the air, dancing in circles. She did a cartwheel, her feet flying above her head, making her dizzy.

She didn't care who was watching. Or even if there was anyone else out there at all.

"I can go out on dates, right?" Angela sipped from a cup of coffee the next morning. *Black. With three or four sugars.* She couldn't say that she exactly loved the taste. But she knew it was one of those things you acquired over time. Like luggage.

"Of course," Angela's mother replied. She seemed a bit taken aback, but she was handling the news okay. "But your father and I have some ground rules. Naturally."

"We do?" Her father looked surprised.

"Like what?" Angela asked.

"You have a curfew. We have to know where you're going and who else will be there, and you absolutely can't drink…And if the boy you're with does drink, then you have to swear that you won't let him drive you home…And of course it goes without saying that we have to meet whoever it is first." She dropped an English muffin into the toaster. "And I guess that's it."

That entire speech sums up my mother. "You have to meet him first? But why? It's humiliating. I mean, this person already means something to me—"

"There's already a person who means something to you?" her father asked. He sounded disturbed.

"Yes!" Angela cried. "And I don't see why you can't just trust me. Why do I have to parade him in front of you?"

"Because. We want to drag you down to our level," her mother replied coolly.

Angela glared at her. As if it weren't hard enough to deal with Jordan Catalano already, now she had to convince him to come to her house to meet her parents?

"Hi." *No. Too cute.*

"Hi!" *Too eager.*

"Hello." *I sound like a salesclerk.*

Angela had been standing in the hallway outside the gym for five minutes, practicing, rehearsing. Why she even needed to think about what to say to Jordan and how to say it seemed completely ridiculous after the night before. But she did.

She kept running the scene between them in the car over and over in her mind, like a movie. She wanted to see Jordan so much, but at the same time, she felt like she needed to be prepared. Especially considering what she was about to ask him. She felt like she had just slipped into an episode of *Beverly Hills 90210.*

That's it, she told herself. *I'll pretend to be Brenda, asking out some guy that Kelly really likes, so it won't seem real, and—*

The door opened, and Jordan walked into the hall, surrounded by his friends. "Oh, hi," Angela squeaked, startled.

"Hey." Jordan stopped in front of her as his friends

dawdled across the hall, obviously waiting for him.

"So, I can't get that song you wrote, like, out of my mind." Angela cleared her throat. *I don't sound like Brenda or Kelly. I sound like me. And it's awful.*

Jordan glanced over his shoulder at his friends. "I'm still not finished writing it."

"Yeah. Well, there's this movie? It's showing this weekend at that place near the university? Anyway, it reminds me of your song," Angela said. "When I heard your song, I mean, it made me want to see the movie again."

"Oh? Well. We could do that, sure…"

"But here's the thing. This is going to sound really weird. But my parents are, like, from the Stone Age, and they want to, like…meet you. Before we could go to the movie." Angela looked nervously at Jordan. She felt like she'd just asked him to marry her.

"Oh."

"I mean, you could just come by or something. Like, tonight. And then it would be settled, and we'd be able to see this cool movie. Like, anytime. This weekend."

"Catalano, come on," Shane called.

Shane, get your own life, Angela felt like saying. *Do you have to constantly be dragging him away? You're like this incredibly annoying anchor or something.*

"So would you want to come over, tonight? Say, around seven-thirty?" she asked Jordan.

"Yeah, okay. Why not?" Jordan said. He waved at her, then took off down the hall with Shane and his other friends.

Angela heaved a sigh of relief. Mission accomplished.

Okay, so maybe it hadn't gone as smoothly as she would have liked, but he hadn't been completely *against* the whole idea, either.

Now if only she could get through the evening with her parents. She wondered what they would think of Jordan. They'd hate him, probably. Just because his hair was occasionally in his eyes, or because he didn't tuck his shirt in right, or because he...never said much.

What if he didn't say much...of anything...when he came over? Like, at all?

"Angela?"

She froze in front of the mirror, mid-spritz. He was here. Like, at her house. Announcing Jordan, to meet Patty and Graham.

"Brian's here for his Malcolm X book!" her mother called up the stairs.

Angela let out a huge sigh. It was only Brian Krakow. And he was only showing up at the most inconvenient time ever, which he had only been doing ever since he was old enough to cross the street by himself.

She grabbed the paperback off the floor and went downstairs. "Here's your book." She tossed it to him. He just barely managed to catch it, since he was carrying his saxophone case in one hand.

Brian stared at her. "How come you look like that?"

"Like what?" Angela replied. She was wearing a cranberry crushed velveteen dress, and she'd put some curls into her hair. Just a couple—nothing drastic.

"Brian, would you like something to drink?" her mother asked politely.

Danielle walked down the stairs. "Hi. I'm ready for my sax lesson."

"Lesson?" Angela asked. Suddenly there was way too much happening around her, as if it were a normal weekday night at the Chase house. It wasn't normal. Nothing about it was supposed to be normal. An event was about to occur. An event with potential historic proportions. "There's going to be a *lesson* here?" She stared at Danielle.

"You did say *sax*, didn't you?" Angela's father asked, sounding uneasy.

"You look like you're going to a costume party," Brian observed, wrinkling his nose. "As somebody else."

Angela felt like asking for the book back, so she could hurl it at Brian's head. "Look, if you must know, Jordan Catalano is coming over, okay?"

"So where should we do the lesson?" Danielle asked.

"What?" Brian asked Angela, completely ignoring Danielle's question. "*What* did you just say?"

"Shut up! Why is that so amazing? I mean, I'm sorry if you disapprove, Krakow."

"It's not that I disapprove. I'm just...nauseated, that's all."

"Likewise, I'm sure. Just please get out of here already, will you guys?" Angela asked. "Have your lesson at Brian's house."

"So, you and Jordan Catalano are, like...a *couple*?" Brian asked.

"Yes! He's coming over. This weekend we're going to see *The Bicycle Thief* together and—"

"Do you actually think that Jordan Catalano will understand one word of *The Bicycle Thief*?" Brian asked.

"Shut up!" Angela cried.

"*You* didn't even understand *The Bicycle Thief* until *I* explained it to you!" Brian yelled.

"That's such a lie!" Angela replied.

"You are bringing that idiot to *The Bicycle Thief*?" Brian went on.

"You *don't* know," Angela told him, her voice quivering with anger. "You could never understand. Not for one second."

"Brian, I'm going upstairs, okay?" Danielle called.

How dare Brian Krakow stand there and call Jordan an idiot! If he only knew...but she wouldn't tell him, or anyone. It was something private between her and Jordan. "You think you understand everything. But you don't. You just analyze everything until it barely even exists!" Angela yelled at Brian.

He glared at her, looking genuinely hurt, then turned and went out the front door, slamming it behind him.

"So...Jordan will be here soon. Right?" her father asked nervously.

"Hey, it's Tino," Shane announced after answering the phone.

Jordan looked over at him. Frozen Embryos were just wrapping up a practice session at the loft.

"There's a party over on Claybourn?" said Shane. "Yeah, okay. See you." Shane hung up the phone and turned to the other guys. "Let's go. I could use something to eat anyway."

Jordan's friends all started picking up their jackets. Jordan strummed a few bars to the song he was still writing, "Red." Some people probably wouldn't understand why that song meant so much to him. Why anyone would write a song about a car.

"Yo, Catalano," Shane said. "Come on."

Jordan looked over at his friends, who were all standing by the door, waiting for him. He could go with them. It would be so easy. "No...there's this thing I gotta do."

Shane stared at him, confused. "What thing?"

"Just…this thing. That I said I would do."

Shane shrugged. "Whatever. Later, I guess."

Jordan vaguely heard them all saying good-bye to him. He felt like he was in another world, sealed into some kind of capsule. Like everything was happening around him, and he was unable to move. A Frozen Embryo.

He could just go. Now. It would be so easy.

No it wouldn't. He didn't meet people's parents. He didn't go to girls' houses. He didn't have anything against the concept, but…he didn't know how to act. He felt like he was being sent to the principal's office or something.

And if he went…what did that mean? Was he obligated to *keep* going, like, as a regular thing? Like school?

He pictured Angela for a second. Then he stared at his fingers on the guitar strings, struggling to get a new chord.

Angela stared at the few random carrot and celery sticks hanging off the edge of the plate, wilted, as if they knew they wouldn't be needed. A few broken tortilla chips lingered at the bottom of the bowl, as jagged as shards of glass. The leftover salsa had a slight film on the top, like the skin on the chocolate pudding at school.

This life has been a test.

If this had been an actual life, you would have received instructions on where to go and what to do.

"We kept it loose. It wasn't definite. It wasn't like a date," Angela told her parents. "It was more like a…thing. A pre-date."

Angela had been sitting in the living room with her parents since seven-thirty. It was now nine-thirty. Jordan wasn't coming. He hadn't called. He was...the lowest form of life on earth. An idiot, maybe, but not because he couldn't read.

"Oh, I know," her mother said.

"Sure," her father said.

"I'm actually pretty tired. I think I'll go to bed." Angela stood up, her legs cramped from being in the same position for two hours straight. Waiting. Like a fool. For somebody who obviously had forgotten all about her.

Or even worse, had remembered, and still not come.

She went upstairs into her bedroom and closed the door. Then she sank onto the floor, her legs giving out what little strength they had left, and she started to cry.

Chapter 9

"I just want to die," Angela told Rayanne the next morning at school.

"More than usual, or like the same?" Rayanne asked. "Because of Jordan?"

"Just because. Life is fatal," Angela complained as they stopped beside Rickie's locker. "Why can't I be more like you? I mean, your relationships might be short—"

"I'll say," Rickie commented.

"—but at least they're real. You're not making it all up," Angela said.

"You know," Rickie said, "you haven't even heard his side yet."

"What *side*?" Angela said. "There can't possibly *be* another side. And I never want to see him again for the rest of my—" And suddenly, mid-sentence, there was Jordan, walking down the hall toward them, like he wanted to chat before first bell. *There he is. Oh my God.*

Angela wanted to run away, but her feet wouldn't move. It was kind of like driving by a horrible car accident. She didn't want to look, but she had to. At him.

She glanced up, and he gave her this pathetic little smile. That was enough. She couldn't take any more. She took off, Rayanne right behind her.

In my humble opinion? People who, like, blow off other people? Shouldn't be allowed back into society. At least not for a couple of days.

"Coffee?" Patty Chase offered Angela on Saturday morning.

"I hate coffee. It's bitter no matter how much sugar you put in it. And it doesn't even wake you up. It just leaves these awful stains on your teeth." Angela drummed her fingers against the kitchen counter.

"Well, that's true, but—honey, not *all* coffee is bad. I mean, you can't judge coffee entirely on one *cup*," her mother argued.

"Mom, don't even try to cheer me up with some weird metaphor about how the right cappuccino will come along," Angela said.

"Okay..." her mother said slowly.

"Because you can't possibly understand. I behaved like a total fool! I let myself believe in something that wasn't even real. I was, like, in love with this fantasy that doesn't even exist." She glanced out the window. In the front yard, her father was tossing a softball to Brian, who tossed it back.

"Why is Dad playing catch with Brian Krakow?"

"I guess living with three women could make any man desperate," her mother commented. "Come on, let's go outside. Maybe some fresh air—"

"—will help," Angela finished. "Mom, you've been saying that forever, and for your information? Fresh air only helps when you've got, like, food poisoning and you're in a car." *Not that salmonella poisoning, which I had once, felt worse than this.*

Angela stepped out the front door. Her father saw her. "Here, you play," he said, and tossed Angela the baseball glove.

Brian gently tossed the ball to her. "So what did your parents think of Jordan Catalano? Were they, like, revolted?"

Angela fired the ball at his chest. "We're not talking about Jordan Catalano. Ever again."

"We're not? Okay, we're not." Brian glanced at her parents, who were sitting on the steps, and threw the ball back to her. "Why not?" he asked tentatively, smiling.

Angela threw the ball. "Because you are incapable of understanding."

"Oh yeah? Why?" Brian asked.

"Because. It's never happened to you. I mean, wait until it happens to you, Brian." Angela suddenly felt superior, in a strange way. As if she ought to have some kind of medal, a reward for the pain she'd gone through. But the only kind of reward was this knowledge that she didn't want to have, that she'd get rid of if she could.

"I cannot wait until it happens to you. Because I am going to turn to you and *laugh*. And say, see? See? I *told* you so."

She threw the ball over Brian's head. But he didn't chase it. He just stared at her.

"So, Jordan wanted me to tell you. He's, like, sorry," Rickie said on Monday morning.

"'World Happiness'! Who thought of that?" Rayanne cried. They were all standing in the hallway at school, outside the cafeteria, looking at the latest posters of social events. There was a new green poster with a globe painted on a disco ball. It announced Saturday's World Happiness Dance.

"Sharon's idea, probably," Angela said. "So what do you mean, he was sorry?"

"He just couldn't make it that night, or whatever," Rickie said. "Something came up. The band, I guess."

Angela frowned at the poster. That was not an apology, as far as she was concerned. Apologies consisted of groveling. Utter penance. Tears. "So are you guys going to this dance?"

"What!" Rayanne shrieked.

"It could be sort of fun," Angela said, shrugging.

"Angela. You're not, like, expecting *Jordan* to ask you?"

"Maybe she just wants to dance," Rickie said.

"Exactly!" Angela agreed. "So wait—there's no way?"

"Angela, Jordan Catalano doesn't *go* to school dances. As, like, policy," Rayanne explained. "I mean, if you wanted to go, which of course you don't, you could always let Brian Krakow take you."

Angela coughed. "Excuse me? But then I'd be, like...at the dance with Brian Krakow! It's not the World *Misery* Dance, it's the—"

"Excuse me? I'm looking for Ms. Chavatal's office." A cute boy Angela hadn't seen before was standing behind Rayanne, looking lost. He had short sandy-colored hair, and cool-looking black-rimmed glasses. He was wearing hand-painted Converse sneakers and a black beret.

"Well…it's down that way," Rickie told him, pointing down the hall. "But she's probably having lunch in the teachers' lounge, because that's what she does. At lunch. Usually."

"Okay. Thanks," said the boy, nodding. "Cool vest," he said, smiling at Rickie. Then he turned and walked away.

"Like, who looks for a *teacher* on their lunch period?" Rayanne scoffed.

"He's new," Rickie said, his gaze closely following the boy as he walked away. "I mean…you can tell."

Between seventh and eighth periods, Angela was in the girls' room, smiling at her reflection in the mirror. Phew. Nothing in her teeth.

"So…the World Happiness Dance. You thought of that, right?" Angela asked.

Sharon sighed, exasperated. "You're not going, either."

"I sort of can't. It's just that Rayanne and Rickie…" Angela noticed that Sharon was looking at her like *So, do you do everything they say*? "Well, it's just not the kind of thing I'm into. I mean, I'm sure it'll be great and everything."

"Oh, of course. It'll be fantastic!" Sharon said. Then she slumped against the sink. "No one's going. No one. I can't believe it. Everyone's acting like they couldn't care less whether they go or not. Like I'm doing this all for my health or something!"

"I'm sure a lot of people will end up going," Angela told her. "That's the way those things always happen."

"Do you think so?" Sharon looked up, her face creased with worry.

"Oh, yeah. People start, like, turning into couples. And then everyone will go." She was saying it only to encourage Sharon, who'd obviously put a lot of work into the dance. But the more she said it, the more she actually believed it.

"Really?" Sharon asked, finally sounding hopeful.

"Yeah, just watch. I'll probably be the only person who ends up not going," Angela said with a shrug.

Then she pictured herself, on Saturday night, sitting in front of the TV with Danielle and her parents, reaching into a bowl of microwave popcorn and watching an animated movie that involved singing and dancing wildlife.

Not that Danielle would pick a movie like that. But her mother would. "It's a family movie," she'd say. "We're a family."

As if she or Danielle could ever *forget* that.

"She looked at me all concerned, wanting to know if I was planning to go to the dance." Rayanne laughed as they walked down the hall after school the next day. "The counselors in guidance are so weird! So I, like, broke down and cried. It was hysterical."

"But, like, how's it really going?" Rickie asked.

"So far, ever since my party—no drinking, no drugs," Rayanne announced. "I'm so clean you could eat off me."

"That's great," Angela told her. "Hey, there's that guy. From before."

"And his cool sneakers," Rayanne said.

Rickie cleared his throat. "So you know that girl, Pam Troy?"

"The one with the heart tattoo on her hand? Who wears crop tops in January?" Rayanne asked.

"Who broke down and cried that time in human sexuality when we were talking about mood swings?" Angela laughed.

"Right. Her," Rickie said. "I was thinking of asking her. To the dance."

"Why?" Rayanne asked.

"Look, maybe the dance is stupid, but—"

"No, I mean...why don't you ask *him?*" Rayanne gestured to the new boy.

"Shut up!" Rickie hissed.

"Well, isn't that who you really want to go with?"

"Yeah. In some imaginary universe, but—"

Rayanne patted him on the back. "Just leave this to me."

"Rickie, you have to be, like, really careful when she says that," Angela said. "Trust me."

"Rayanne! If you say one word to him about me?" Rickie threatened. "I will kill you."

Angela smiled. It was fun, worrying about someone else's love life for a change. She was glad Rickie had found someone to like. Even if, for a couple of minutes, she'd thought about asking that new guy herself.

"And his name is Corey," Rickie told them. "Just, you know. In case you were wondering."

"Hi." Angela walked up to Jordan, who was leaning against his car. It was right after school, and she couldn't stand not getting this over with before the day was finished. She wished there was some kind of time limit on emotions—sort of like classes. A bell could ring at the beginning and at the end. That way you'd know when to stop feeling bad, like...officially.

"Hey," Jordan said.

Apologize. Apologize. Grovel. "So, did you hear about that thing? That they're going to exterminate tomorrow?" Angela was trying to sound casual, but her voice kept squeaking.

"I didn't hear that," Jordan said.

"Oh. It's, like, some kind of large rodent, I guess." Angela waited a minute for Jordan to say something else. Then she asked herself why she was bothering. He never did. And he definitely didn't believe in formal apologies. She hated him for that. But she liked him too much to hold it against him.

"People obsess about the weirdest things. Like this World Happiness Dance? What does that even mean..." Angela realized she was babbling, but she just couldn't help herself. "Like if we all dance together, the world will be happy? Come on. Like, I seriously doubt it."

Jordan tossed a cigarette butt onto the ground. "There's a dance?"

Rayanne was right, Angela thought. "Yeah. There are about five hundred neon posters up around school. I doubt I'm even going, though. I mean, I'm sure you're obviously not going." She looked over at him.

"See, I have this philosophy." The cigarette butt was still burning and he squashed it with his shoe.

Angela was stunned. "You have a philosophy?"

"I don't make plans," Jordan explained.

You make them. You just don't keep them, Angela wanted to say.

"If I go somewhere and someone I know is there? Cool. There's something...natural about it," Jordan said. "But once you start making plans then you have, like, obligations. Which suck. My feeling is, whatever happens, happens."

Or not. Angela nodded. So that was why he hadn't shown up the other night. He didn't make plans—didn't believe in obligations. It had nothing to do with *her* at all. "I really respect that...philosophy," she told Jordan.

Jordan shrugged and got into his car. As he started the engine, he glanced up at her, standing by the car door. He looked like he was about to ask her if she wanted a ride home. She wanted him to offer her a ride.

But he just looked at her, and then stared straight out the window. Maybe offering her a ride home meant making plans. Maybe she ought to just...show up in his front seat someday.

"Well, I left my geometry book in my locker, so..." She shrugged.

Jordan moved the gearshift on the column to Drive and pulled out of the parking lot.

"Rayanne's right. You should ask Corey to the dance," Angela told Rickie on Wednesday. They were sitting outside school on the steps, eating lunch. Angela was trying not to notice that Jordan was standing a few flights up, hanging on to an extremely pretty girl's every word. Corey was sitting on the grass, painting somebody's Jack Purcells.

"I can't ask him. Anyway, you don't understand—it's not that easy. I mean, you couldn't know," Rickie said.

"Oh. You're so right, Rickie. I could never understand having an obsession with someone that I have a negative chance of ever becoming involved with. That situation is *completely* beyond my comprehension."

Rickie smiled. "Okay, so you made your point. We're surrounded by people we could never have."

"Look at them," Angela said. "Leading their happy

little fun-filled lives. But you know...we don't need them, Rickie."

"We don't?" Rickie asked. "I mean...you're right, we don't! We are people in our own right. Tragically *lonely* people, but—"

"But we have each other, don't we? I mean, just because we're not going to that stupid dance." Angela shrugged. "Big deal. 'World happiness.' Right."

"Angela, maybe we should go!" Rickie said.

"Oh my God, Rickie! We'll go *together*. That way we won't be alone." Angela grinned.

"It's perfect. I feel *so* much better now," Rickie said. "You know? Just to know that it's settled and we're—"

"Hey. See you Saturday."

Angela whirled around. It was Corey. He was standing on the steps behind her, looking at Rickie.

"Excuse me?" Rickie asked.

"Rayanne said that we were going to hang together at the dance. Did I get that wrong?" Corey looked confused.

"Oh. No," Rickie stammered. "That's right. She did say that."

"Cool. So...Saturday." Corey turned and walked back up the steps, into the school.

Angela looked at Rickie, who was staring at Corey. "Wow. So Rayanne actually did something."

"The truth is, as much as I'd never admit this to Rayanne? This is why she's such a good friend."

"Yeah." Angela thought about the things Rayanne had set up for her and Jordan. They hadn't worked out exactly right, but she'd gotten a lot further than she would have on her own, sitting around and thinking about doing something. "So." Angela shrugged. "I guess I should just go with you and Rayanne and Corey, right?"

"I guess," Rickie said. "Except it might seem like you and I are together? Like boy-girl together...like a double date or something."

"Oh yeah. It could."

"Whereas if it's just me and Corey and Rayanne...no, wait a second—that's too obvious, isn't it? So maybe you *should* come."

"No. I shouldn't. You're right," Angela said. She looked around the lawn and tried not to panic. So everyone else was going to the dance, just like she'd told Sharon they would. Even Rayanne, who hated school-sponsored events. And maybe even Jordan, only he just couldn't *plan* to go, because he was philosophically opposed to plans. Whereas when she didn't have plans? She would end up at home, watching *The Lion King*.

Then she spotted Brian Krakow.

"So I guess, in conclusion...that I can't, like, study twenty-four hours a day, so...all work and no play or whatever—"

"Brian? Are you asking me to the dance?" Delia Fisher asked. She was looking up at Brian, who was standing on the steps outside school. They were sharing a Big Guy apple pie.

"Um. Yeah," Brian said.

"Okay, great," Delia said, smiling. "I'll have to ask for the night off at Big Guy Burger, but that shouldn't be a problem."

A date, Brian thought. *I actually have a date. With somebody I like.*

"So you'll pick me up on Saturday or something?" Delia asked.

Brian was about to answer when Angela walked over

and stood right in front of them. "Hi!" she said cheerfully. "Can I, like, talk to you for a minute? It's kind of an emergency."

Angela took a step closer to him, and he noticed her hair. How it smelled incredible. It reminded him of an orange grove he had passed when he was visiting his grandmother in Florida...when he was *eight*.

"We were sort of—" Brian began.

"No, it's okay, I have to go anyway," Delia said, stuffing her half-eaten lunch back into a blue nylon lunch bag. "See you Saturday?"

"Um. Yeah." Brian smiled awkwardly. There was something very strange about having Angela and Delia in the same area at the same time. Like, too many hormones.

"So you, like, asked her to the dance?" Angela asked.

"Yes. You know, I wanted to go with someone, so I just thought—*her*. And I just asked. It was pretty simple. She seemed pretty much blown away." He shrugged.

"That's great," Angela told him. "Look, this is going to sound really weird. I know you're already going with Delia, and I'm really happy for you, but Rayanne's doing this thing...for Rickie? So they're, like...reserved. And I was just thinking that since we're neighbors, it would be sort of convenient, I mean, if there's any way that I could just...go along with you guys."

As Angela continued to babble, Brian realized that something truly amazing was happening. When you stripped away all the blathering, Angela Chase was actually asking *him* to the dance.

"Just to, like, get me there," she quickly added. "Not that we'd actually be going together."

"Of course," Brian said.

"'Of course'…is that a yes? Because I don't want to, like, *go* go, I mean, you're going with Delia. I just need a technical way to actually get there," Angela explained.

Brian sighed loudly. "It's not a problem. I mean, fine. Tag along or whatever."

Angela smiled at him, and he tried not to notice the way the sun was glinting off her red hair, or the way her blue-gray eyes had this innocent, helpless look.

So he had asked Delia to the dance, and now Angela was asking him. *What cruel irony*, Brian thought, feeling his stomach begin to ache. *Can something be so ironic that it makes you want to puke?*

Or maybe it's just the Big Guy apple pie.

"What did you do? Invite Corey to the dance—with you and me? When I specifically asked you not to!" Rickie said.

"Yeah." Rayanne chuckled.

"Rayanne, listen to me," Rickie said insistently. "This isn't funny."

"It isn't?" Rayanne asked.

"You've driven me crazy in the past, but I was willing to overlook it. And the truth is, I want to go. But if you say one word to embarrass me while the three of us are together—" Rickie threatened.

"She won't," Angela said.

"Angela's right, because I won't even be there," Rayanne announced.

"What?!" Rickie cried.

"Well, I'm just not sure if I'm ready to go to an event like that. My counselor said I might not be able to handle it—"

"Who cares about your stupid drinking problem?" Rickie interrupted. "This is my *life*!"

"Relax, it's not a problem," Rayanne said with a shrug.

"Yes it is!" Rickie insisted. "And I think I should know because it's, like, my life."

"I'll call Corey. Okay? I'll explain the whole thing. Don't worry, it'll be fine," Rayanne told him.

"Not to worry you or anything, Rickie?" Angela asked. "But the last time she said that...she lost that letter of mine in the Natural History Museum."

"And look how that turned out," Rickie said.

"Great," Angela sighed.

"Terrible," Rickie said at the same time.

Angela came down the stairs on Saturday night, wearing her red velveteen dress over a black scoopneck bodysuit. She'd dressed up a little, because it was fun. And in case Jordan just happened to show.

The first thing that hit her when she walked into the living room was Brian's tweedlike blazer. His neat shirt and ironed pants. Brian actually looked...almost good.

"Where's Delia?" Angela asked. "Are we picking her up?"

"So wait a second. Your Dad is picking you two up, right?" Mrs. Chase asked. "Or is it three of you?"

Brian was staring up at Angela as she came down the stairs, a goofy expression on his face. "As it turns out? Delia can't go." He clasped his hands together.

"Really?" Angela's mother asked.

"Wait a second. Why not?" Angela asked, stunned.

"It's...her aunt. She's, you know, in the hospital."

Somehow Angela didn't believe that.

Brian smiled, like, a little *too* happily. "So, should we go?"

Rickie rolled up the sleeves of his bright blue jacket. He and Corey were sitting in the bleachers overlooking the Liberty High gym, which was adorned with smiley faces pasted onto hanging globes and signs that said:

WORLD HAPPINESS DANCE.
DANCE FOR WORLD HAPPINESS.
BE HAPPY—DANCE!

The basketball floor was sparsely dotted with people dancing, and a huge ring of other students watched.

Rickie laughed. "So finally, the mouse runs across the classroom and I swear to God, starts, like, *chasing* Ms. Shindelheim," he told Corey. "Which is when she tripped over Nicholas Cahill. Which is why she has the neck brace."

Corey cracked up laughing, tilting the black beret on his head. "You're, like, *really* funny."

Rickie smiled. Everything was going so well, he hardly felt like himself. Could he really be happy—at the World Happiness Dance? Was Sharon Cherski *that* good at organizing?

"So," Corey said, looking around the gym for what seemed like the hundredth time. *He's just nervous, like I am*, Rickie told himself. "Where's Rayanne?"

Rickie looked down at the bench seat where his feet were propped. "She didn't call you?"

Corey shook his head. "No. Why?"

"Well, she told me she was going to call you.

Because, see, like...she's not coming," Rickie said.

"Why?"

Rickie shrugged. "It's kind of a long story."

"Oh," Corey said. He looked completely disappointed.

He came here because of Rayanne, Rickie realized. *Not me.*

So why are we even sitting together?

"Lot of people," said Brian.

"Yeah," said Angela.

"Wow."

"Yeah."

Angela scanned the room desperately for Rayanne, for Rickie, for Corey...for Jordan. Not that she was planning on looking for him, but if she *just happened* to see him... "Hey, do you think you could get me something to drink?" she asked Brian.

"Um, okay, what do you want?"

Angela shrugged. "Whatever." Brian walked away and Angela scanned the gym again, searching for a familiar face. There was Sharon, in the middle of the room. She was surrounded by Kyle and his friends, who apparently all thought it was necessary to wear their letter jackets in order to make the world happy. She saw Rickie walk away from Corey over to Brian and start talking to him while they both ladled punch. She wondered what had happened with Corey. She wondered if Jordan was ever going to show up, or if he already had.

When you don't make plans, you miss people.

"It's punch." Brian was back. He held out a cup of red liquid that looked more like cough syrup.

"Thanks. So what did Rickie want?" Angela yelled

over the blaring dance music.

"Nothing." Brian shrugged his shoulders.

Angela glanced over to where Rickie was standing, beside the punch bowl. He looked upset, as if he'd rather be anywhere else. "What did you say to him?" she pressed.

"Nothing. I just said...you know, that maybe it was better if he didn't hang out with us tonight."

"What?! Rickie's my *friend*. Why wouldn't I want to hang out with him?"

"He's my friend too," Brian said. "It's just...what if we wanted some privacy or something?"

"Privacy? Why would we want privacy?" Angela set her cup of punch down on the bleachers.

Brian shrugged. "Well, we probably wouldn't, but—"

"Brian, what do you think is happening here?"

"What?" Brian glanced at the shiny floor. "Nothing."

"Didn't I explain the whole reason I came with you?"

"Yeah, but I just thought, what if we wanted to dance or—"

"We're not going to dance!" Angela cried.

"I *realize* that. Look, it wasn't some big *plan* or anything. I mean, I don't even believe in *making* plans. Whatever happens, happens."

Angela glared at him. "That is the stupidest thing I've ever heard in my life!" Just then she spotted Delia. Delia Fisher. She was making her way through the crowd, toward the side of the dance floor where Sharon and Kyle were standing. Delia was *here*, not at some hospital. Brian had lied, Angela realized. To her and probably to Delia too.

"Brian, what did you say to Delia?"

Brian looked nervously around the gym, as if he hadn't known Delia was coming, either.

"You don't understand people, Krakow," Angela said. "You are so heartless!"

She stood up and started walking across the gym toward Delia, to say something, anything, to apologize for not doing anything except asking for a ride, and—

There was Jordan. Standing underneath the basketball hoop, surrounded by his friends. *We didn't make a plan, and it worked*, Angela thought, feeling breathless as he looked up and saw her coming. He stared at her for a long moment, his eyes traveling over her body in the way that Angela hated when anyone else did it. He was chewing a toothpick while he stared at her, smiling slightly, as if he were possibly happy to see her.

Then Shane punched his arm, and he turned away from her, as if she didn't even exist.

"So Rayanne never called Corey. And when I told him she wasn't coming? He was, like, depressed. Disappointed. Like even if he and I had been having a good time together until that moment? It didn't even matter because Rayanne wasn't coming and he was, like, looking forward to that. Obviously. God, it was *so* obvious."

"I'm sorry," Angela said. She had come outside to look for Rickie—and to get away from Brian and Jordan. "You know what? We should just kill both of them."

"That's a good idea. But the truth is, that would only solve half of the problem." Rickie sighed.

"What's the other half?" Angela asked.

"The other half is...me. You know, the fact that... I don't fit." Rickie pulled his coat around him. "I belong nowhere. With no one."

Looking at Rickie, Angela felt even worse than she had when Jordan blew her off a few minutes ago in the gym. Because Rickie was really hurting, and it had nothing to do with anything superficial. It was almost too real. Even if she told him that he belonged? She'd be lying. Because sometimes she didn't even feel that she herself belonged. To anything, or any place, or anyone.

She reached over and wrapped her arms around Rickie, pulling him close to her. They just stood like that for at least a minute, squeezing each other tightly.

The gym door opened, and Jordan walked out. His friends kept going past her and Rickie, while she watched him anxiously, breaking apart from Rickie. Jordan stopped a few feet away from her. *Oh my God*, Angela realized. *He's actually waiting for me.*

She glanced at Rickie, not sure what she should do. Rickie might still need her, but there was Jordan, and he'd practically never waited for her in his entire life. It had always been the other way around.

"It's okay," Rickie told her. "Go."

Angela smiled and nodded. As Rickie made his way back into the gym, Angela turned and moved toward Jordan. "Hey," she said softly.

Jordan took a few steps closer, looking so intensely at Angela that she felt completely overwhelmed, as if he knew some secret about her. Or some secret way to get to her heart. She retreated a step toward the fence and tried to catch her breath.

Jordan put his hands on the fence, on both sides of her.

Angela was aware of her heart beating. Of her lungs contracting and expanding. Of her whole body responding. He couldn't be any closer unless he was actually going to kiss her. And he had to, now, or—

"Why are you like this?" he whispered, his breath warm on her cheek.

"Like what?" Angela asked softly, her voice nearly gone.

"Like how you are."

In the parking lot, a car horn honked. Jordan gave her one last, incredibly seductive look, then walked away.

"How am I?" Angela called after him, her entire body still tingling. "How am I?"

But Jordan didn't turn around. She heard the car door slam, and then the squealing of tires as Jordan and his friends peeled out of the parking lot. She couldn't even move for a few minutes. She just stood there, wondering how it was humanly possible to stand that close to someone and not have touched or kissed them...and yet feel like you had.

Angela tapped Brian on the shoulder. "Hi. I'm back." He didn't turn around. She leaned closer to him and said it again, so he could hear her. She noticed he was distracted. That his gaze was glued to the dance floor.

A loud dance song was pulsating out of the speakers. Angela followed Brian's gaze to the center of the gym. Delia and Rickie were dancing together. *Really* well. Like they'd been dancing together their whole lives, and like they'd never stop.

"Brian," said Angela, close to his ear, "this was all my fault, and...I can't even explain why I asked you to take me here, but...I'm sorry for ruining your night," she apologized.

Brian didn't reply. He was still staring at Delia and Rickie. Most everyone in the gym was.

"These things are so stupid," he finally said.

"I know. No one ever has a good time." *Except Rickie and Delia. Some people know how to make the best of things*, Angela thought. Right now, they weren't worried about what anyone thought of them, or even what they thought of themselves. They were living the moment. The way she hadn't just done with Jordan outside.

Why am I like this? Angela wondered. *Why can't I just get out there and dance, instead of thinking and worrying about it?*

But, watching Rickie, she knew he had something she didn't. He could abandon himself. Leave parts of his life that maybe he didn't like sitting there on the bleachers while his body danced wildly. He could throw himself completely into the moment.

Out there on the dance floor...it's like belonging doesn't matter. Because right now, the way Rickie's dancing and everyone's watching? He belongs to everybody.

"Do you use orange shampoo?" Brian suddenly asked.

Angela looked at him. "No."

"Oh," Brian said.

"So, you want to...I don't know. Dance or something?" Angela asked Brian.

"Not with you," he replied, staring at Delia. "I mean...I just don't feel like it. I guess I don't care about dancing that much."

"Oh. Me neither," Angela said with a shrug.

Chapter 10

In the basement, near the north exit? There's this place, where certain people go. For only one reason. And it's this unwritten law, like gravity, that it's the only thing that can happen there.

The boiler room. Angela had always thought of it as a vague destination for janitors, or a place where horror movies were set, because it was overheated and cramped and there was no exit. Things exploded down there, or threatened to. And it was fenced in, like a strange prison cell for bad furnaces. What exactly *was* a boiler, anyway?

Now the boiler room was where she and Jordan made out. It had just sort of...started one day, when he left her a note to meet him down there. Now they met there constantly. Between classes. After classes. During classes. During lunch, even. Her whole life had been divided into Kissing...and Not Kissing. And Kissing.

Every night I make the same vow. That tomorrow I will

go to geometry review. Because I'm about to flunk a major exam. But every day...

"I'm missing my geometry review." Angela stared into Jordan's eyes, his lips met hers again. "Luckily it's optional."

They barely ever talked when they were in the boiler room. So when they did, it seemed incredibly meaningful. Like they had only just discovered language, and didn't really need it yet, except for things that related to each other.

"There's a tiny leaf in your hair," Angela said.

"Where?"

She reached and pulled it out, and they started kissing again.

"Was that your stomach or my stomach?" Jordan asked a few minutes later, when they finally separated.

Angela touched her lips. They were beginning to get puffy. "I don't know." She couldn't remember the last time she'd eaten. Her parents had been bugging her daily about her nutritional imbalance. As if she could even focus on antioxidants and dietary fiber.

"Hey, Catalano! You down here?" Shane's voice rang out in the stairwell, echoing off the concrete basement walls.

Angela and Jordan let go of each other. "Shh..." Jordan whispered. Angela looked at him, puzzled. "The fact that we come here? Let's keep it, like, our secret," Jordan said.

Too late, Angela thought. *I already told Rayanne and Rickie.* "Why?" she asked.

"No reason," Jordan said casually.

"Catalano!" Shane yelled.

Sometimes I wish that Shane would transfer to another school.

Jordan took a last glance at Angela, then turned and ran out of the boiler room and up the stairs. Angela collapsed against the chicken-wire fence, being careful not to let it squeak.

"Hey," she heard Jordan say to Shane, who was apparently standing at the top of the stairs.

"Who you got in there?" Shane asked.

In there? Like it's a cage or something. Angela wrapped her fingers around a corner of the wire. *And I'm like...a zoo animal. Or a bird.*

Or a prisoner.

"Just a girl," Jordan said. Then Angela heard the door open and close, and they were gone.

He hadn't said it loudly, but the words seemed to reverberate up and down the empty gray stairwell. *Just a girl.* That was all she was? But she was...Angela. Chase.

She picked up her jacket and ran up the stairs after them. When she came out into the hallway, they were already half a locker bank away, laughing and shoving each other. *Just two boys.*

"Once again, if you received lower than a seventy on this quiz, you should be attending my fifth-period review sessions!" Ms. Lerner announced as she walked around the classroom, returning graded quizzes.

Angela glanced at the clock. Only a few more minutes and she'd be with Jordan again. She watched Ms. Lerner nervously.

In geometry I feel like a criminal. I've missed every single review session. So I try to be invisible.

It's surprisingly easy. You just sit in the back and keep quiet and let the boys shout out all the answers. Which they will, even if they're wrong. Boys aren't as afraid of being wrong, for some weird reason.

Ms. Lerner stopped in front of Angela and slapped her quiz down on the desk. Angela looked at all the red marks on her paper, and the 59. She hadn't even broken 60. That was like getting every other question wrong. She glanced up at Ms. Lerner, but her teacher wouldn't even look her in the eye.

It's that bad, she realized. She'd always done okay in math before, and she knew Ms. Lerner knew that, because that was the reason they kept all those "permanent records" in the first place. She'd spoken to Angela a few times already about "not working up to your potential."

Is there some kind of test for potential that I shouldn't have done well on? Angela wondered. *It gets really tiring, trying to live up to something that...you don't even know you have, or where to find it.*

"Good job," Ms. Lerner said, handing a corrected quiz to Abyssinia Churchill, who sat next to Angela. Angela glanced at her paper—she couldn't help herself. 98. Abyssinia had almost gotten 100.

The bell rang, and Angela hurriedly started getting her things together. "Angela Chase!" Ms. Lerner called out as she started to leave the classroom. Angela paused in the doorway. "How do you expect to pass the upcoming exam?"

Angela shrugged. "I'm really sorry."

"Sorry won't cut it," Ms. Lerner said. "I want to see you at tomorrow's review. Is that clear?"

"Yes," Angela said, backing out the door. "Okay."

There was Kissing...and there was Not Kissing.
And then there was geometry...and not doing geometry.

"You should consider having your lips frosted permanently," Rayanne said that night. She was over at Angela's house, working on applying a frosted lipstick they'd bought that afternoon.

"They feel like they were," Angela said.

"Yeah, I noticed. They look all...used. But in a good way."

"Don't tell anyone, okay? That I've been meeting Jordan in the boiler room," Angela asked.

"Why?"

"Because he doesn't want people to know about us yet, or something. So he wants to keep it—us—a secret." It sounded even more dumb when *she* said it, but Angela couldn't take it back.

Rayanne put the cap on the lipstick and set it on the counter. "Not for nothing? You're letting Jordan Catalano, like...control you."

"What? I am not!" Angela protested. "I don't believe this. For months you've been trying to convince me to do all these things that I would never even dream of doing. And now that I'm actually doing them, you think it's wrong. I mean, haven't you made out with guys in the boiler room?"

"So?" Rayanne shrugged.

"So, are you letting them *control* you?" Angela felt like she and Rayanne were on *The Ricki Lake Show* all of a sudden.

"No, Angela, they don't control me. Because as I have told you a billion times, I don't let myself get *involved* involved. I am the type of person who can handle the boiler room," Rayanne said proudly. "You, on the other hand, are not." She put on her jacket.

Angela stared at her. "Well, sorry. I just thought maybe you'd be happy for me after everything we went through."

"I am happy for you." Rayanne picked up her bag and stuffed her makeup kit into it. "But, well, you know."

I know, Angela thought. *Nobody is ever that happy for someone else, really. They just say they are.*

"Catalano!"

Angela snuck around the corner of the boiler room, pressing herself back behind a large metal object as she heard footsteps coming down the stairwell. *It's like this adult version of hide and seek.* She peeked out and saw Jordan putting breath drops in his mouth.

"Catalano?" Shane called into the grayness.

"Oh…yeah?" Jordan finally replied.

"In your own world much?" Shane asked. Angela could hear Shane's boots as he clomped down the stairs. "So, you hear about Buffalo Tom being at Pike Street Friday night? Tino found out. It's like…an unannounced thing."

"Oh, yeah?" Jordan asked. "Buffalo Tom? Well…sure. Yeah. We'll go. Okay."

"Yeah, so…oh, okay. Later." Shane walked off, and once the stairwell door shut, Angela quickly opened her geometry textbook and held it under the faint red of the emergency light.

She glanced up as Jordan slipped into the boiler room. "I have all this geometry to…review."

He came over to her. "I was hoping you'd be here," he said softly.

Angela gently dropped her book onto the floor. That was the nicest thing Jordan had ever said to her, by far. She was about to kiss him when she stopped herself. "So you're going to Buffalo Tom on Friday night?"

"What?" Jordan looked stunned. Angela couldn't blame him. It was the first time they'd ever talked *before* kissing.

"Buffalo Tom. Didn't I hear that they're playing at Pike Street?" She studied his reaction. "I mean, I think I heard that somewhere."

"Oh, yeah. I'm going," Jordan said. "Why?"

The boiler made a grinding noise, as if someone had accidentally dropped a wrench into it. Angela shrugged. "No reason."

That afternoon, on her way to science class, Angela ducked into the girls' room. When she opened the door, she almost keeled over. Rayanne and Sharon were actually talking. To each *other*. In friendly-sounding tones.

Some things are, like, physically impossible. Or they should be.

"Don't you have French in, like, two seconds?" Angela asked Sharon.

"You should talk," Sharon replied. "How come you're never at geometry review?"

Angela shrugged. *Because I'm in the boiler room. Loving it and hating it. And myself.* She touched her lips, remembering.

"Angela...we're, like, concerned, okay?" Sharon said.

"What? Because I cut a few geometry reviews?" She laughed harshly. "So you guys, like, *discuss* me now?"

"No!" Sharon cried. "We don't discuss anything."

"We're not even *friends*," Rayanne said. "Are we?"

"No!" Sharon insisted. "It's just that we were talking about Jordan and you and—"

"Look, I am *not* discussing Jordan Catalano with you," Angela declared.

"Why is he keeping you two a secret?" Sharon asked. "Angela?"

"How do you know that?" Angela asked.

"Rayanne told me," Sharon said.

Angela could barely believe it—Rayanne was confiding in Sharon now? *Why?*

"Look, we're only talking to each other like this because we care about you," Rayanne said.

Those are the weirdest words a person can hear. To be discussed...because people care? How is that "caring"?

"Hey. When I was drinking and taking drugs too much—"

"Which was, like, all the time," Sharon interjected.

Rayanne looked straight at Angela. "You wanted me to stop, right? As my friend?"

"Wait—you're not comparing me and Jordan to you having your stomach pumped, are you?" Angela said.

"You don't see the connection?" Rayanne asked. She looked at Sharon. "Because it's there, right? I mean, the connection is..."

"Self-respect," Sharon said.

"Thank you." Rayanne grinned and slapped Sharon's hand in a high-five.

This isn't happening, Angela told herself. *Sharon Cherski and Rayanne Graff are not, like...coming together. For my benefit. Like I need a...group effort.*

"Angela, the point is, who is he to treat you like this? I mean, what? You're not cool enough for him to be seen with you?" Sharon asked. "I mean, please! It's really clear.

You deserve *so much* better."

Angela finally found her voice. "You know, just because he's not Kyle and he doesn't parade around school holding my hand—"

"I don't even get this holding hands thing," Rayanne interrupted. "What is, like, the point?"

"And if he doesn't want to be seen with me, how come he just asked me to meet him at Pike Street Friday night to hear Buffalo Tom?" Angela went on. Sharon and Rayanne both looked stunned...almost as stunned as Angela felt for just having lied. "Not that I could go, because I have to study all that geometry."

"Maybe I'll go," Sharon mused. "I really like Buffalo Tom."

Angela and Rayanne both stared at Sharon. "Really?" they asked in unison.

"What? I'm not allowed to like cool bands?" Sharon asked, looking offended. "I'm so sick of being...perfect all the time. I mean, I broke up with Kyle. I have a total right to screw up my exams!"

Rayanne nodded. "More like an obligation, really."

The weirdest part about asking Brian to come over Friday night to help me study for my exam? Is that I actually believed that I meant it at the time. When I basically knew that I'd be standing right here, at Pike Street, looking for Jordan.

She could just picture Brian showing up at her house at precisely nine o'clock, and getting all disturbed because she wasn't there. When really, all he had to do was walk back across the street.

Then she remembered that she'd given Brian her textbook so he could review what *she* was reviewing, because he had taken geometry in the first grade practically and was now in calculus.

"I can't believe I'm even here," Sharon said as they moved through the crowd around the bar toward the stage, where Buffalo Tom was playing. "I have so much work to do."

"He's not here," Angela said. "We may as well just leave." She scanned the crowd again.

"I can't believe you want to leave! Like you couldn't have a fun time, just because *he's* not— Wait a second. There he is." She pointed to the pool tables off in a corner, where Jordan was crouched over, making a shot.

When he finished, he stood up and, directly facing them, glanced around the club. Then he turned and walked around the table to take his next shot.

Angela could have sworn that he saw her. Hadn't he? But maybe he wasn't expecting her to be there. After all, they weren't supposed to make plans...but here she was, and there he was...so why couldn't he just come over? "He doesn't seem like he saw me. So, anyway, he's busy. I'm not going to—"

"Forget busy," Sharon said. "He asked you to meet him here. Right?"

"I mean, why isn't he, like, coming over to *you*?" Rayanne demanded.

"Because," Angela said. *Because he doesn't want to. Because he didn't invite me, I invited myself.* "He doesn't see me! He's busy!"

"Look, will you just go over there?" Rayanne said.

"Exactly!" Sharon agreed. "I mean, really. You're *supposed* to meet him here."

Angela glanced over at Jordan. *Please come over here. Please spare me the humiliation of having to go over there.*

Somehow having both Rayanne and Sharon there made everything worse. If he didn't talk to her, everyone was going to know how it really was between her and Jordan. All of her different versions of herself were going to know the truth: that he didn't want to see her, unless it was in the boiler room. And that he wanted to keep it a secret not for *their* sake or her sake, but for his own.

Taking a deep breath, Angela walked over toward the pool tables. "Hi," she said nervously.

Jordan focused on the position of the cue ball on the table, lining up his next shot. "Hi."

Angela glanced at Shane. He smiled at her. Not a nice smile, but sort of superior. Jordan sank the next ball, and started to move to the other side of the table. Angela followed him. "So..." she said.

He looked up from where he was leaning on the table. "You're kind of crowding me."

Angela stared at the striped balls on the green felt, her eyes filling with tears, blurring the numbers. She started backing away, and watched as Jordan knocked a ball into the corner pocket. The ball rattled as it sank down underneath the table and rolled toward the end.

Angela took a step toward him, looking him right in the eye. "You know—" *You're a really terrible, horribly mean person. Do you know that? Do you know anything...about people? At all?*

But she couldn't find the words. They were too awful. How could you tell someone that they were supposed to act nicer toward you? That ruined the whole point.

She looked at Jordan one more time, then turned and walked away.

* * *

There's something about Sunday night that really makes you want to kill yourself. Especially if you've just been made a fool of by the only person you'll ever love and you have a major geometry exam on Monday. Which you still haven't studied for, because you can't, because Brian Krakow has your textbook. And your little sister is finished with her homework. And that creepy 60 Minutes watch is making you feel like your whole life is ticking away.

Angela was lying on the couch, watching television and thinking about how this had to be one of the worst weekends she had ever had, when the doorbell rang. She slowly pulled herself off the couch, which took almost all the energy she had left.

"I don't believe you," Brian said as soon as she got the door halfway open.

"I know," Angela said.

"I came over on Friday night and Danielle told me you went to see some band." Brian walked into the house and threw her geometry textbook onto the couch. "You *asked* me to come over. You *asked* me to review a bunch of chapters! You're in some kind of dream world, you know? That, like, revolves around you, all the time. You have no concept of anybody else's life—"

"I know," Angela said sincerely. "And I'm really sorry."

"You can't even begin to imagine the kind of pressure I'm under," Brian said, pacing around the living room. "You think you're under pressure because of one lousy exam? You? That is, like, so laughable!"

"Brian, you're *completely* right." Angela fidgeted with the drapery cord. "You've never been more right. Okay? But...could you please just explain geometry to me anyway?"

"Are you completely insane?"

"Yes, I probably am," Angela admitted.

"You think I care? You could not possibly conceive of how much studying I have to do tonight. Have you even *heard* of calculus?" Brian went on. "Geometry is a paid vacation compared to calculus. And I'm, like, in accelerated. Do you realize the pressure on a person when it's assumed that they'll get an A? 'Oh, Brian, you'll just get another A.'" He mimicked his mother's voice. "*You* have the option of insanity. *I* do not. And that is what drives me really crazy."

"Oh." Angela tried to take this all in with a straight face. But if she were Brian? She'd be happy to be in accelerated calculus. Because it would mean that she'd gotten past geometry. "Well...what if—"

"I have to leave," Brian said abruptly. "I'm leaving."

Angela stood by the window and watched Brian walk down the driveway. So that was that. Her only hope of passing? Gone. Across the street. Deserted by Brian Krakow.

And it would be all Jordan's fault when she failed.

Or my own fault. For choosing Jordan over studying.

Angella,
Meet me in the Boiler Room. Okay?
Jordan.

Angela stared at the tiny piece of paper that had fluttered out of her locker when she opened it. After the way he'd acted on Friday night, did he actually expect her to just show up as usual, like nothing had happened?

But Angela knew, in her heart, that she had to go. If only to find out what he could possibly say. Then she'd have to decide whether her life would keep being divided into Kissing and Not Kissing...or whether it would be Not Kissing and *Really* Not Kissing.

Not Even Thinking About Kissing. That's the stage I need to get to, she thought as she descended the stairs.

This time, Jordan was standing in the shadows, waiting for her. He gave her this soulful look, the way he always did right before he kissed her. Then he put his hand on her shoulder and she stepped up against him, pressing her lips against his. He kissed her the same as always, as if nothing had changed, as if she were still his favorite person on earth.

Angela pushed him away. "Don't say hello or anything."

Jordan swallowed. Angela pictured his stomach, a pool full of breath freshener drops. "Hello," he said blandly.

"I can't believe I came here. Why did you ask me to come here?" She threw the note onto the floor and stared at him. "Why are you like this?"

"Like what?" Jordan looked confused.

"Like how you are!" Angela cried.

Jordan shrugged. "So leave."

Angela turned to go, then stopped herself. "First admit it."

"Admit what?"

"That...I exist. That all of this down here *happened*. That you have emotions, and you can't just treat me one way in front of your friends, and then leave me some private *note* that's the exact opposite!" She paused, but he said nothing.

She picked her backpack off the floor. "And by the way. I spell my name with *one* L," she said with a mixture of anger and disgust, then she strode out of the boiler room and up the stairs.

She thought about the time Rickie had decided that he couldn't keep hanging out in the girls' bathroom, and how he'd walked around saying good-bye to everything. That's what she felt like doing now. *Good-bye, chicken wire fence. Good-bye, rumbling boiler that sounds like it needs an inspection. Good-bye, weird smells and red emergency lights.*

Good-bye, kissing.
Good-bye, Jordan.

"'My mistress' eyes are nothing like the sun...'"

Jordan stared at the sheet of paper on his desk. Mr. Katimski was reading the poem printed on it out loud.

"'Coral is far more red than her lips' red; / If snow be white, why then her breasts are dun...'"

At first, Jordan tried to follow along, matching the lines to the spoken words, but then he gave up and just listened.

"'If hairs be wires, black wires grow on her head,'" Mr. Katimski continued, barely glancing at the page, as if he had the sonnet memorized. "'I have seen roses damask'd, red and white, / But no such roses see I in her cheeks; / And in some perfumes is there more delight / Than in the breath that from my mistress reeks....'"

Jordan blinked, staring at the back of the girl who sat in front of him. Angela wasn't in class today. She never missed class. At least, when Jordan showed up, she was there. Always.

"'I love to hear her speak, yet well I know / That music hath a far more pleasing sound; / I grant I never saw a goddess go— / My mistress when she walks treads on the ground.'"

Jordan wondered whether she was skipping class because of him. Because she didn't want to see him, maybe. *What would that be like? Angela avoiding me. Starting today.*

"'And yet, by heaven, I think my love as rare / As any she belied with false compare.'"

Jordan found himself thinking about those last lines that Mr. Katimski had just read.

"What kind of girl is Shakespeare describing?" Mr. Katimski asked, looking around the room.

Nobody said a word.

"Well, is she the most beautiful girl?"

"No," Brian Krakow said softly.

"Is she a goddess? Physically perfect? One of those girls who stops traffic when she walks down the street?" Mr. Katimski went on.

"No," Brian said again.

"So," Mr. Katimski said. "He's not in love with her?"

"Yeah," Jordan said, without thinking about how he would sound, or whether the answer was right. "He is."

"Why?" asked Mr. Katimski, looking at Jordan. But he didn't have an answer. It was Brian who spoke up.

"Because she's got, like, flaws. She's not some untouchable fantasy girl—"

Yeah, thought Jordan. *That's the answer.*

"—she's real."

"Okay, and if the two parallel lines are cut by a transversal, then what happens?" Abyssinia Churchill asked.

Angela thought about it. "The angles are congruent?"

"That's it!" Abyssinia said, smiling.

Angela was starting to feel better about the exam,

which was only happening in about five minutes. And about herself. Abyssinia had been nice enough to help her cram for the exam for the past forty-five minutes in the girls' room, while she cut English class, and even though Angela wasn't going to ace the test, she wasn't going to bomb it, either.

Suddenly Sharon burst into the girls' room, a huge smile on her face. "You guys! The copy machine ate our geometry exam! It's postponed until tomorrow!"

"Yes!" Angela and Abyssinia shrieked, leaping off the radiator and hugging each other.

"Lerner's having one more review session this afternoon," Sharon announced.

"I will *definitely* be there," Angela said.

"You'd better be," Abyssinia said, raising her eyebrows.

Angela laughed as the three of them walked out of the girls' room. Right away, she saw Jordan, standing across the hall with Shane and his friends. She stared at him for a second, frowning, then she forced herself to look away. Looking at him wouldn't change anything, she knew. It would only make her more sad.

She turned to Rayanne, who was standing by some kind of sign-up sheet. But Rayanne wouldn't look at her—she was staring at Jordan, as if he had suddenly sprouted a head of Chia-Pet hair.

Angela turned to Sharon. "What's going on with her?" she started to say, but before she could finish the sentence, Jordan left his friends and came walking straight toward her, crossing the hall.

He stopped in front of Angela. "Hey. Can we...go somewhere?"

Angela looked at Jordan, stunned for a moment. She

tried to measure what he was really asking her.

He blinked, waiting.

"Sure," she told him.

Then Jordan Catalano did something that Angela thought he never would. He actually reached out and put his hand in hers. Right there. In front of her friends. And his friends. And everybody.

It feels strong and soft at the same time, thought Angela as he interlaced their fingers. *And it's not even clammy. It's like...the perfect temperature. Of course. What else would it be?*

She looked up at Jordan and smiled faintly as they started walking down the hall. So this was what it felt like. To be recognized. To parade down the hallway holding hands, for everyone to see. She was now becoming all the things she'd said she hated about Sharon.

And it felt *wonderful*.

"Angela?" Rayanne called. She sounded the way Mrs. Chase had when Angela rode her bicycle down the street for the first time without training wheels. Like she was proud and afraid at the same time.

"Wait—don't forget the geometry review!" Sharon yelled to her. "We have to work on some more proofs!"

There are proofs? And then there's, like...evidence, Angela thought, touching Jordan's palm.

She could always study that night.

Or next year.

Chapter 11

"Hey, slow down!"

"I can't!"

Angela jerked the car to a stop in the school parking lot. "Sorry. You shouldn't have let me, I mean, it's only my second time—"

Jordan reached across the seat and pulled her closer, giving her a mammoth kiss. They'd been together—like, officially together—for about a week now, and life was good. No. Beyond good. For Angela, life had never felt better. When Jordan released her from the kiss, Angela forgot she was supposed to be driving. Or in a car.

"My second time behind the wheel," she finished. "I'm sorry. I just couldn't remember which was the brake."

Jordan was giving her this look, like he didn't accept her apology. "How long are we supposed to keep doing this?"

He sounded serious, like maybe he wasn't talking

about her informal lessons from Catalano's House of Driving.

"I don't know what you mean," Angela said.

Jordan moved closer to her again. "Yeah, you do."

"Well, I mean, yeah, of course I do, but...what do you want me to do? I mean, I know what you want me to *do*, but..."

"Can't we just...you know?" Jordan breathed into her ear.

"Just...do it? Right here? In the parking lot?"

"In the car," Jordan argued.

Angela laughed. "Right. I'm sure we'll just do it here, right now."

"Why, where do *you* wanna do it?"

"I don't know—no, wait! How about tonight, in my room—after my parents fall asleep! Yeah, that sounds perfect. We'll have to be really *quiet* though." She laughed again. But Jordan didn't seem to think it was half that funny. "Do you really expect me to choose a place?" she asked him.

"Well, yeah," Jordan said automatically.

Angela nodded. "I better go to geometry." *Pick a place? To...just do it? Who am I, anyway—Rayanne?*

"You guys signed up for the Drama Club? *Why?*" Angela asked Rickie and Rayanne later that day. "You guys don't care about *activities*. You don't even know what they are."

"Katimski kept asking me, like, every other minute," Rickie said. "It was getting pathetic. Besides, I think Corey's doing it."

"Yeah, it's stupid, but I figure maybe it'll get us out of something," Rayanne declared. "Besides, I was talking with my counselor, and she said the Drama Club could count as, like, points. On my *permanent record*," she whispered in a dramatic voice.

"Your permanent record must be, like, a thousand pages long," Angela said with a laugh. "So who were you guys trashing when I came up?"

"Cynthia Hargrove. You know, she has that nose stud that's so small it looks like a pimple?" Rayanne commented.

"She's such a sleaze. You're a major improvement," Rickie declared.

Angela's heart dropped. "What do you mean? Jordan went out with her? With Cynthia Hargrove? She's, like, a junior."

"Went out? I don't know about that. I mean, I don't know how many locations they actually *went out* to," Rayanne said.

"Okay..." Angela said slowly. "So, she's someone that Jordan used to...um..."

Rayanne nodded. "Yes. Exactly. Jordan used to *um* her."

"You knew that, right? You must have known that," Rickie said. "I mean, even *I* knew that!"

"Oh, sure," Angela said. "I mean...I didn't quite know everything, about Cynthia Hargrove. But now I do. So!"

So now what? Jordan and Cynthia had sex. So I can't stop thinking about the fact that people everywhere—including Jordan—had sex. That they just had it. Cynthia. Rayanne. My teachers. My parents. She shuddered. Everyone but me.

That night at about eleven, Angela was opening a jar of mustard to put on her sandwich when she heard a scratch against the kitchen window. She dropped the lid. "Who's there?" She went over to the door and pressed her ear against it. Somebody was definitely rustling around in the bushes. Or something.

Maybe it's a raccoon in the garbage, she thought.

She slowly pulled the curtain on the door to the side and peered out into the night. Two eyes looked back at her and she almost collapsed.

"What are you doing here?" she whispered, opening the door.

Jordan walked into the kitchen like it was something he did every day. "Hey. Wow…food." He picked a slice of bologna out of its plastic wrapper.

This is a dream. I'm having a dream, Angela told herself. *I've had this dream before…but it didn't involve cold cuts.* "You know, it's really late. My parents are *right* upstairs."

Jordan sniffed the bologna and put it back. "They are?" He walked over and put his hands on her waist.

"Well, they do live here," she said.

"You said you wanted to do it in your room while they were sleeping…" Jordan whispered into her ear.

"I was *joking,*" Angela said. "Seriously. You have to go."

"Okay," Jordan said. He pulled her closer and kissed her intensely, for what seemed a long time.

Angela touched the back of his neck, running her fingers through his hair, as she kissed him back.

"So, you know that empty house over on Cloverdale?" Jordan asked when they finally broke apart. He brushed at a crumb on her lip.

Angela heard the unmistakable sound of one of her parents' feet hitting the floor upstairs. Somebody was up.

From the sound of the footsteps, she guessed her mother. "Shh!" she told Jordan, trying to hear if her mother was simply going into the bathroom or—

"The house that's been for sale for, like, thirty years?" Jordan continued in a low voice. "Tino told me there's a way to get in, through this window in the back? So people have been going there to...you know. So you want to go? Friday night?"

"Wouldn't we be, like, breaking and entering?" Angela asked, trying to squirm out of Jordan's grasp.

"It's just...this house. So we can be somewhere." Jordan kissed her again.

"Angela?"

Angela jumped backward, almost hitting her head against the wall. "Mom?" She hurried out of the kitchen toward the staircase.

Her mother was coming down the stairs, a white robe wrapped around her silk pajamas. "Didn't I predict this?" Patty snapped. "Didn't I say that this would happen?"

Angela stared at her mother, smiling weakly. She had no idea how to respond.

"Didn't I tell you that if you skipped dinner, you'd be hungry later?"

Angela laughed nervously. "Right. Yeah. Listen, Mom?"

"Look, I'm not trying to interfere," her mother went on.

You have no idea how much you're interfering, Angela thought. *It's not just a sandwich...it's my life.*

"It's just that I think it's important for us to all eat dinner together, as a family. And by the way, I expect you to help me and your father with Thanksgiving dinner this Thursday. Your grandparents will be coming and your Uncle Neil will be here too."

"Oh, sure," Angela said, nodding. "No problem."

"Good. So, finish up whatever it is you're nibbling on in there, and please remember to clean up." She started back up the stairs. "And don't forget what we talked about tonight, about how Daddy and I still need to meet your friend Jordan."

Angela winced. "I won't forget."

"Sweetheart, don't be embarrassed. You like this Jordan person. I have no problem with that—we just want to meet him!"

Would it be possible for her to talk any louder in her own house, after eleven P.M.? Does she think that I can't hear her? Actually, Angela practically couldn't hear her mother, over the beating of her own heart. "*Okay*, Mom, good night," she muttered.

Jordan was eating a rolled-up slice of turkey when Angela went back into the kitchen. "So. You like me."

Angela felt her face get hot. "Shut up."

"Your mother says you like me, so…"

Angela hit him on the arm. "Shut *up*."

"So Friday night?"

"Oh. The house. Right."

"There are, like, eight bedrooms," Jordan said.

Vacancy, Angela thought, picturing a flashing neon light on the old, abandoned house. *No vacancy*. "That many?"

He smiled and kissed her. Angela felt herself hesitating, like she wasn't sure whether to kiss him back or not. She wanted to, desperately, but then…she couldn't get her mind off this house, with its empty, used rooms. And how people would be, like...waiting. For her and Jordan's room.

"Well. See you." Jordan grabbed another slice of turkey and went out the door.

Closing the door, Angela leaned against it, her face resting on the glass windowpane, cooling her cheek.

"I'm returning your mom's chafing dish. And you're supposed to tell her thanks from my mom."

Angela nodded, taking the silver-plated dish from Sharon Cherski. It was Friday morning and Angela stepped onto the porch. She was never happier to see her friend. "Sure. My mom's coming down in a minute. She's taking me to get a flu shot."

Sharon frowned. "I hate shots. Well, see you." She started to leave, but Angela stood in front of her. She needed somebody to talk to about this. And it definitely wasn't her mother.

"So...how was your Thanksgiving?" Angela heard herself asking lamely as she set the chafing dish on the porch railing.

Sharon shrugged. "Okay. How about yours?"

Angela shrugged too. "Okay. Same as usual." *Quit stalling.* "So...I heard you and Kyle broke up?" Angela knew she would get to the point eventually. These things took time, she rationalized. "Was there a reason?"

Sharon tapped her chin with her forefinger. "I guess it was...my beliefs. I decided that I couldn't go against them. I didn't feel like I should give them up, even for Kyle."

"So how did you...I mean, did you just tell him? That you wouldn't have sex with him?" Angela asked eagerly.

"Oh, no. We had *sex*," Sharon said. "My belief? Was that he was being a butthead. Which was sadly true."

"Oh." *Even Sharon.* Angela leaned back against the railing, nearly bumping the chafing dish into the bushes below. "You had, like…"

"Constantly," Sharon said with a wave of her hand.

Angela smiled. "That's great." *But now I don't have anyone to, like…confide in.*

"Dad?" Angela asked on Friday night. "Can I talk to you?"

Mr. Chase walked out of the living room toward Angela, who was hovering in the kitchen doorway. "Well, I met him," he said. "He seems…well, anyway, what does meeting somebody prove?" He smiled, lifting the lid off a pot and checking inside.

"Dad? Um…" *How exactly does one ask to be grounded?*

"You want to meet Hallie? One of my students from cooking class? And her fiancé, Brad?"

Angela shook her head. "Not really. Dad, it's just that…maybe I shouldn't go out tonight. With Jordan."

"Why?"

"Because. Mom's not here, and she said you both had to meet him before I could—"

"No, it's okay. Your mom got held up at work. It's not like you didn't try to do the right thing. Don't worry about it. I'll explain it to her."

"Really? Will that work?" Angela asked. Her parents didn't always agree on the parenting thing.

"Sure. Honey, it's okay. Really," said her father.

"Oh." Angela nodded. "Great."

Thanks, Dad. Do you have any idea what you're so happily sending me off to? In the living room, she could see the soles of Jordan's shoes propped up on a leather hassock. *Make yourself at home much?* she thought.

Her dad had actually met Jordan Catalano...and he hadn't hated him. Anything could happen now. But she still wasn't sure she wanted it to.

"Are you sure we won't go to jail or something? If the cops, like...burst in?" Angela crawled through the window of the deserted house later that night, catching her coat sleeve on a splintered edge of the window frame. She wondered how many people had come to this house for the same reason she and Jordan were now here. And how many other girls had lost their virginity because of the slow real estate market.

Jordan unhooked her sleeve and helped her through the window. "Cops never really burst in."

Angela dropped from the counter to the floor. "They don't?" She glanced around uneasily. There were about seven or eight kids in the kitchen, drinking beer and talking in the shadows. The house was lit by a few candles, a fire hazard waiting to happen. "What if the neighbors report us?"

"Then we'll leave," Jordan said with a shrug. He took off, leaving Angela standing next to the refrigerator, feeling painfully obvious. She walked through a doorway, into what must be the dining room. A group of girls standing in the corner turned in unison to examine her.

The way they were looking at her, smirking and giggling, Angela felt like she had a sign stamped on her forehead: VIRGIN.

Then she noticed that Cynthia Hargrove was one of the girls. *I don't belong here*, she thought. *I'm not ready to become...one of those girls. Not that anything's wrong with them, but it's just not me, I don't think.*

"Angela?" Jordan said softly, standing behind her. "There's, like, no empty rooms now. So..."

Angela glanced over at Cynthia and just as quickly looked away. "So what do we do?" she asked Jordan. *Can we leave?*

"See, I was wrong. There's only, like...three bedrooms."

"Oh." Angela nodded.

"Someone told me there were eight. But there's three."

"Right. Three."

She and Jordan sat down on an old, debilitated couch in the living room. Angela drummed her fingers against the arm and started humming. She felt as anxious as she had when she was waiting for her flu shot that morning...only she didn't have any old issues of *People* magazine to read.

"I'll be right back," Jordan told her, getting up almost as soon as they sat down.

Angela shifted on the crumbling couch cushions. *Now what? How does one casually wait for, like, the most important moment of her life?* She was kind of hoping that the neighbors would report them to the police—but if they did, it would have to be soon. Very soon. Before—

"Oh my God! Rayanne!" Angela jumped off the couch as Rayanne walked right past her, toward the kitchen.

"Wow. You're here?" Rayanne sounded shocked.

"Yeah, I..." Angela didn't know what to say, only that she wanted to talk to Rayanne. She *needed* to talk to Rayanne.

"Well, I'm kind of, like, on my way out. Tino's giving me a lift, so I gotta go now—"

"But wait. Rayanne," Angela pleaded, trailing behind her.

"I seriously can't stay. He'll leave without me. That is *so cool* that you're here with Jordan. I'll call you tomorrow!" Rayanne waved over her shoulder on her way out the kitchen window.

Angela watched Rayanne's feet slip through, noticing the worn soles of her granny boots. It would be so easy to just...leave.

"Hey." Jordan touched her sleeve. "There's an empty room now. So—"

"I'm, uh, kind of worried," Angela said, looking at him. "I mean, about Rayanne."

"Didn't she just leave?"

"*Exactly*," Angela said. "And see, I know how she's not supposed to drink anymore. And just now? When she was leaving? She looked really out of it. So I think I'd better, like, go after her." She knew she was babbling, but she couldn't stop herself.

Jordan stared at her, blinking his eyes a few times, as if he'd been caught in a bright spotlight and his pupils were still adjusting. "So go," he said coldly.

As she climbed out through the window, Angela knew she had just done something that she couldn't take back, but that would change her relationship with Jordan forever.

And in a way, it had nothing to do with sex at all.

Chapter 12

If there's anything worse than a Sunday night? It's a Monday afternoon. About three o'clock. When the week has started and there's, like...no end in sight.

Angela lay on her bed, staring at the ceiling. She'd come home early from school, claiming she was having a bad reaction to Friday's flu shot. But it wasn't the flu shot. She just couldn't face Jordan. How could you tell somebody like Jordan Catalano that you weren't going to sleep with him, when that was all you'd wanted for months? She was having a bad reaction to her own cowardice. If that's even what it was.

Just because everyone my age is supposed to know about sex, and be ready? Does that mean I'm abnormal if I'm, like...not?

"Honey! Sharon's here!" her father called up the stairs.

Angela rolled over, pressing her face into the pillow.

She didn't want to talk to or face anyone. She felt hideously embarrassed.

Sharon knocked three times on the door, then opened it. "Angela? You're not really sick, are you?"

"No," Angela said, her voice muffled by the pillow. "How did you know?"

"Rayanne said that you'd...developed symptoms. Like, all of a sudden. When you saw Jordan," Sharon explained.

Angela sighed. Did everyone at Liberty have to know the absolute truth? Didn't anyone believe in privacy anymore?

"So I brought over something," Sharon said. Angela turned over and sat up. "Here." She handed Angela a videotape.

"*Dr. Linda Shields's Guide to Better Loving*?" Angela laughed. "Oh my God. Where did you get this?"

Sharon giggled. "My parents. They've been watching it for, like...a decade."

"So...wait," Angela said, trying to figure out what Sharon was trying to do here. Did she actually think a tape would help? Then again, what did *Angela* know? Maybe it would.

"Come on." Sharon pulled Angela up off the bed. "We'll watch it in your parents' room."

"I'm Dr. Linda Shields. And what I'm about to show you is the true story of several married couples who came to me because they wanted more out of—"

Sharon fast-forwarded the tape. "This part's really boring. Okay. Here we go. Shelly and Mitch." She stopped the tape.

Angela stared at a man massaging oil into a woman's back. Some kind of new age music was playing as Dr. Shields's voice narrated, "Being close means understanding each other in a new way. It means accepting each other's differences, emotionally, physically—"

"So...why did you bring this over?" Angela asked Sharon.

"I don't know. Why were you asking me those questions about me and Kyle the other day?" Sharon replied. "I mean, didn't you want to know because...you and Jordan...never...."

There's this dividing line, between girls who've had sex and girls who haven't. And all of a sudden, Sharon's on one side and I'm on the other. And we both know it.

"Look, you're allowed to ask me things," Sharon said. "Like, in case the tape doesn't quite—"

"What things would I ask you?" Angela said, annoyed. She knew *how*. She just didn't know *why*, or *when*. But she felt like she could ask Sharon anything. She didn't feel that way around Rayanne. "So, did you and Kyle use something?"

"Of course! Angela, you have to. Promise me you'll make him wear a condom if you decide to do it!" Sharon said, sounding like she had just stepped out of a public service ad.

"Okay!" Angela laughed nervously, surprised by Sharon's intensity. "Let's stop talking about it." But she couldn't. There was still something she wanted to know. She and Sharon had grown up together, played together...it would only make sense if they were remotely on schedule with other things. "So what made you decide to, like...go through with it?"

"I told Kyle I wanted to wait until I was ready,"

Sharon said. "And then one night? I totally was." She paused. "But the weird part is that once you do it? You can't, like, go back. I mean, it's just expected. And it kind of didn't matter to him anymore whether I wanted to…or not."

Angela picked at a square in her parents' quilt that was coming undone. "So. Did you feel different? Afterward?"

"This is going to sound really dumb." Sharon laughed. "But I looked at myself in the mirror afterward, just to see if I looked different." She looked at Angela eagerly. "Do you think I do?"

Angela studied Sharon's face. Same brown eyes. Same incredibly healthy pink skin without one blemish or scar, the kind of skin you saw in magazines. Same expression. "No," she told her honestly.

Then they both laughed.

"You should talk to Jordan," Sharon suggested. "About this. Because you have this tendency? To, like…shut people out."

Angela thought of how mean she had been to Sharon, just blowing her off a few months ago because she all of a sudden wanted to hang out with Rayanne. How she had never offered an explanation. "I know," she said softly.

Suddenly, Angela heard footsteps on the stairs.

"Quick!" Sharon said. "The tape!"

Angela sprang off the bed, ejected the tape, and tossed it to Sharon, who slid it under the bed just as her father walked into the room.

"Dad! Where's that…thing?" Angela asked, trying to sound innocent. "That Mom told me to give to Sharon to give to Camille?"

Her father looked from Sharon to Angela to Sharon,

completely dumbfounded. "That thing?"

"Maybe we should check your room again!" Sharon said cheerfully.

Angela and Sharon left the bedroom, then ran downstairs, laughing. When they went out the front door, they stopped abruptly, as if it weren't funny anymore. Brian was riding his bicycle around the street, doing figure eights.

"Well, bye. See you tomorrow," Sharon said. "Don't forget to get that...*thing* later."

"Right," Angela said. "See you." She felt like she wanted to thank Sharon, but that seemed weird, so she walked over to Brian instead. "Um, Danielle has my bike. And so I was wondering..." She shook her head, realizing what she was just about to do. "No, forget it. I'm sorry."

"What?" Brian stopped circling and stared at her.

"I was going to ask if I could borrow your bike." Angela kicked at a dead leaf on the sidewalk. "But forget it. Because I'm, like, always doing this, always asking you for stuff and then not giving it back, like this sick habit. And just because you're always polite about it, doesn't mean it isn't totally selfish on my part, and so I'm just not going to do it again. Okay? I've made up my mind."

Brian got off the bicycle and looked at her questioningly. Like she had just told him that his bike was covered with some kind of radioactive material. He looked at the seat, then back at her, as if he were trying to decide whether she'd fit.

Angela reached over and took the handlebars. "I'll have it back by tonight."

Okay, so I have this problem making up my mind. But I meant it...when I said it. It's just that I have to talk to Jordan. Like, this minute. Before I lose my nerve.

Jordan was leaning over, nearly hidden under the propped hood of his red convertible, his flannel shirt draped over the engine. He was concentrating so much that he didn't seem to hear Angela coast to a stop in front of him. At least she hoped he hadn't heard—otherwise, that meant he was simply choosing to ignore her. Which was entirely possible, considering the way she'd taken off the other night and hidden from him since.

"Hi." Angela propped the bicycle against the garage. "I'm sorry about Friday. I had just had this flu shot and—"

"Quit lying," Jordan said abruptly. He slammed the hood closed. "Tino told me. Rayanne's been clean for, like...weeks. Right?" He didn't look at her.

Angela scuffed her sneaker against the concrete. How totally awful and embarrassing to be caught in a dumb lie. Why had she even bothered, when the truth was right there in front of them? "Yes," she admitted.

"I mean, you can think what you want about me, like how sometimes I didn't always do the right thing or whatever. But I never *lied*. I can't believe it. I let you drive my car."

Angela's stomach felt like it was being twisted into a tight braid. "It's so hard to explain. It's not going to sound right, because..." Her voice wavered. *Don't cry. Do not cry. Not in front of him.* But she had that crinkling feeling in her throat, and every word she said only made it worse. "Part of me really wants to. But..."

Jordan tossed a rag on the ground. "This is the whole reason I didn't want to start this in the first place."

"Why, because you knew you wouldn't get *sex*? So you'd just be wasting your time?"

"Because you don't get it, okay? You're *supposed* to.

It's what you're supposed to do, like everyone does it. Unless you're, like...abnormal."

Abnormal?

In my humble opinion? That is not a word that should be applied to anyone. Least of all someone you almost had sex with.

Angela stared at him, her eyes brimming with tears. She brushed them away, then backed up a few steps, until she turned completely around and started walking away.

Only she felt more like crawling, as if she'd just been wounded in battle. Jordan had taken a shot at her. He hadn't missed. And he didn't care whether he hurt her, or whether she was all right.

"I can't believe you let Brian look through my backpack." Angela pressed her forehead against the mirror in the girls' room.

"You left it on the *bus*, okay?" Rickie argued. "And the driver, who, like, calls him Curly, returned it to him. And he wasn't *trying* to look in it, but he tried to jam it into his locker and your sex tape fell out."

"It's actually Sharon's," Angela said, her breath fogging the mirror. "The tape, I mean."

Rickie laughed. "Yeah, right."

Angela turned away from the mirror. "Rickie, I *had* somebody. To be with. You know?"

"I know." Rickie stopped combing his hair and gave her a sympathetic look. "I can't even imagine it."

"I feel so stupid!" Angela cried. "My *entire* relationship with Jordan Catalano has totally sucked. And now it's over! Because of me! I should have just had sex with him. I mean, why not? It would have been so simple."

"But...maybe it shouldn't be. So simple," Rickie said softly.

Angela looked up at him.

"I mean, not that I know what I'm talking about, at all. Because I've never experienced it or whatever. But even if I did meet the perfect person?" Rickie stared at his reflection in the mirror and brushed a piece of lint off his shirt. "I just think it should be like...a miracle. Like seeing a comet or something. Seeing the other person's perfectness. Or something. And if you do it before you're ready? How are you going to see all that?"

The toilet flushed, the gurgling water echoing in the almost-empty room.

"Not that I would know," Rickie said with a shrug.

The stall door opened. Angela nearly fell over. It was Cynthia Hargrove. *Cynthia Hargrove* had just heard her admit she couldn't have sex with Jordan. This was too humiliating to even stand. She felt another bad reaction to her flu shot coming on.

"What you said?" Cynthia brushed a tear off her face. "That is so beautiful. That's exactly what it's like." She moved forward to the sink as if in a daze, and started washing her hands. Neither Angela nor Rickie moved.

Cynthia tore a brown paper towel off the roll and turned to Angela. "I know we don't know each other or anything, but could I just ask you something?"

Angela swallowed. Something like: *How could you not have sex with Jordan Catalano?* "Sure."

Cynthia peered into Angela's eyes. Angela focused on the tiny silver stud in her nose. *It does look like a pimple*, she thought. "Did you ever work at Big Guy Burger?"

Angela almost collapsed with relief. "No. Sorry."

Cynthia looked puzzled, but she just shrugged.

"Okay. Whatever." She adjusted the purse on her shoulder and walked out of the girls' room.

"Ex*cuse* me?" Angela practically doubled over with laughter. "She wants to know where I *work*?"

Brian pressed the Chases' doorbell insistently. He hoped Angela opened the door. He didn't feel like explaining yet again to her parents *why* he was there to see Angela. Why did he have to keep coming up with reasons, anyway? Couldn't he just show up, like, unannounced? For once in his life?

Angela pulled the door open, a questioning look on her face.

Brian walked past her into the house. "What do you think? That I don't, like, need my own bike, which I ride, like, all the time? And you can just leave it all over town or whatever?" He shoved Angela's backpack onto a chair by the door as she wandered over to the stairs and sat down. He marched up to her.

Something isn't quite right with her, he thought. She had this look on her face. Like she didn't care if she left the house ever again. For any reason.

Brian sat a few steps down from her on the stairs. "So, don't just take that from me. Yell back at me," he urged. Angela didn't look at him. "I mean, did something...obviously, something happened."

"Nothing happened," Angela said. "Not to me. I just think it's kind of sad. About boys."

"What about boys?" Brian asked.

"How they only care about...you know. Getting you into bed."

Brian cleared his throat. *Is she, like...trying to taunt me? Or does this just come naturally?*

Angela glanced up at Brian. "I mean, don't they?"

"Not *all* boys," Brian said. *There must be one guy who doesn't think like that. And I also happen to care about calculus.* "So...what? Is that, like, a problem you're having?" he asked.

Angela nodded. "Uh-huh. I mean, sure. I think about it all the time, but—"

"Wait, you *think* about it? All the *time*?" Brian exclaimed. He felt like Angela had just told him that Yale wasn't going to accept him, that physics didn't matter in the real world, that up was down...Angela Chase sat around and *thought* about sex. "Like, how often? *Constantly* or..."

"Brian!" Angela smiled. "Yes, shut up. Boys don't have a monopoly on thinking about it."

"They don't?"

"*No*," Angela told him.

"Hmm." Brian didn't know what to say. He was still recovering from the shock. "Okay," he finally said, standing up. "Well...I still want my bike back."

Angela was about to head back up to her room so she could listen to that Cranberries song that always made her feel superior for suffering, when there was a knock at the door. Did Brian expect her to go get his bike right now?

She opened the door slowly. It wasn't Brian. It was Jordan. She looked at him. Her heart felt pierced straight through.

He was leaning against the door frame, like he knew that would get to her the most. "I brought your bike back. Or whoever it belongs to. That guy across the street said it was his." He walked past her into the house and started wandering around, looking at the photographs on the walls.

"It is his bike." Angela closed the door and followed Jordan over to the stairs. "So, are we supposed to say something official?" she asked tentatively.

"You don't have to say anything," Jordan said.

But Angela knew that she did. She needed to explain herself. "It's sort of like...when you let me drive your car those times. And I loved driving...when I wasn't supposed to. It made me feel really powerful. But also really terrified. Like I wasn't ready...for that much freedom."

Jordan cleared his throat and stared at the floor. "Well, you should know, I won't hold it against you. I mean, if your name ever comes up. Or like, when I remember you."

Angela bit her lip. "Thanks."

Jordan shrugged. "No sweat."

Angela felt like the floorboards were coming apart, like she was about to fall straight through. Only she knew it was her legs that were about to give out. She looked at Jordan. "Because it is a big deal. Because sex is, like, the beginning of your life, you know? And sex and death are both—look, I'm not saying that they're the same, but they have the same kind of...Of course, I've thought about having sex with you, constantly, but God! I've never thought about killing you—"

"Okay, okay! Stop!" Jordan said. "Look, at least...you got in some driving practice."

Angela sighed. *So this is what good-bye feels like. A real good-bye.* "Yeah."

"Just...you know. Don't take your turns too wide," he said, then he shrugged and gave her a little smile. "I'm sure you won't."

Sometimes someone says something really small...and it just fits right into this empty place in your heart. And you can feel it settling in there, maybe for the rest of your life.

"Your hair?" Angela said quietly, staring at him. "The way it's really soft in the back. I'm really going to miss that."

"Yeah."

"So...this is it. Good-bye, I guess."

"Bye." Jordan stopped leaning against the stairwell. "See you tomorrow."

Angela walked to him. She wrapped her arms around his waist, and he held her close. Standing on her tiptoes, Angela kissed Jordan as intensely as she could. Like it was for the last time. Like she needed Jordan in order to breathe.

She finally stepped back and let go of him. He nodded once, then headed straight for the front door. Angela followed him, half dragging her feet.

After he left, she closed the door and peeked out the glass frame. As he got into his car, she let out a loud sigh.

She had thought that she would want to die when she and Jordan broke up. That she would feel completely horrible, and abandoned. But she didn't. She didn't feel too great about it or anything, but she didn't feel like her life was over, either. After all, she had simply—in a weird way?—stood up for herself. Done what she believed in.

She wasn't abnormal. She was...herself.

People always say how you should "be yourself." Like your self is this definite, definable thing, like a toaster or something. Like you even know what it is or how to be it.

But that afternoon, she did know. And it was something...someone...she actually liked.

Chapter 13

Angela walked down the hallway to grab her lunch from her locker. Christmas and Chanukah decorations covered the walls, courtesy of Mr. Janosik's art classes, and there was a buzz in the air. That strange energy that came before a holiday, when everyone was counting the days until the big break.

But Angela didn't feel the excitement. She felt like one of those stupid cartoon characters. Sunny holiday cheer was everywhere around her. But over her, there was this relentlessly dreary rain cloud.

Angela smiled weakly at Sharon as she passed her in the hallway. She was wearing her red Santa hat for the yearbook staff's holiday party. *Perfect*, thought Angela, as she reached her locker. But before she could touch the combination dial, Jordan's hand slipped around her body. He twirled to the right numbers, popping open the locker. Then his hand settled naturally on Angela's waist.

Excuse me? Didn't we just break up like...yesterday?

Okay, so maybe it had been ten days, but still. She pulled her lunch bag out of her locker and closed the door. Jordan took his hand off her waist and leaned against the wall, looking forlorn.

Excuse me? But you are not allowed to lean within, like, a hundred yards of me. I have a restraining order.

"What's wrong?" Angela asked. *I mean, I know what's really wrong. You need me. You must have me as your own. You can't live another second without me.*

"Nothing." Jordan sighed. "It's just...I could kill Tino, you know?"

Angela leaned against the lockers, next to him. She knew she was about to do something she definitely shouldn't do. She'd read articles about situations like this. You were supposed to stay far, far apart, have zero communication, try to forget his phone number, and *especially* not let him put his hand on your waist, under any circumstances.

"Do you want to, like, go outside or something?" she asked him.

Angela was sitting on the front seat of Jordan's car. The engine was running and the heater was keeping out the December cold.

Jordan leaned back against the long seat, only a few inches away from her. "...so Tino just said, 'This isn't working out for me,' and then he threw his mike right into Joey's drum. Then he left." Jordan took a drag off his cigarette.

Angela sifted through the carrot sticks in her plastic bag, looking for the best one. "So he *quit*? Tino quit Frozen Embryos?"

"Yeah, and now we have to, like, change our name,

because it was Tino's idea. It totally sucks." Jordan frowned.

Angela shoved aside the thought that he was in more pain over his band breaking up than he'd been over breaking up with her. "I'm really sorry," she said, reaching out and rubbing his shoulder lightly. *I am just so low. I'll find any excuse to touch him.*

"I can't even, like, face rehearsal tonight," Jordan went on. "There's going to be this big empty hole where Tino used to be."

"I'm sorry. But I'm sure it'll work out somehow. I mean, you'll find someone, eventually." *For the band. To replace Tino, not me.*

"Yeah. I guess," Jordan said, putting his hand on top of the hand she was resting on his shoulder.

"Well, I should probably go. I have English next and I need to do some reading." *And if I don't leave right now? I will completely melt all over your car seat.*

That's what it's made of, right? Girls you've melted?

Transition. That was the word Angela's mother kept using. "Honey, this is just going to take a while. Breaking up with someone is a big transition."

So Christmas, like, came and went in a flash of red foil wrapping paper and the usual family parties. And, all of a sudden it's, like, New Year's Eve, Angela wrote in her journal. *Everyone's making these resolutions, like they don't do that every day and then just give up. But here are mine, in writing, so maybe I'll stick to them:*

> *To be less introspective.*
> *To not think about and analyze everything to death.*
> *To stop helping Jordan with his homework.*

To make this transition…transist. Transpire. Happen.
And stay that way.

Angela wondered what everyone else was putting down for their resolutions. Or if some people were smarter and just didn't bother making them.

RICKIE

To find some place where I, like, really…belong.

And to stop wishing that Corey would paint my sneakers. Even if he might want to, I can't ask, and it's just gotten way too embarrassing to hang around him ever since that World Crappiness Dance when Rayanne didn't show up.

RAYANNE

To quit drinking. Again. Because the last time didn't work, even though everyone thinks it did. I mean, those things don't just, like, magically *work*. Just because you *say* you want to stop, that doesn't mean you can. Or should, even. Because maybe it's a part of your identity, and if you give it up, then who are you?

Screw it. I'm calling Tino. Maybe he has some beer.

BRIAN

To never ask Angela Chase for anything ever again, even if it is mine and she borrowed it and technically ought to return it without me going over there and asking for it.

And to not care whether she likes someone just because he drives an old red convertible and has these brief moments of lucidity that she apparently confuses with genius.

SHARON

To get Kyle out of here before my parents get home from their party. To *really* break it off with him. And to never watch a Brad Pitt movie with him again.

Because life is too short, you know? You can't just stay with one person, especially when it's Kyle, and he doesn't support you the way he should, like he doesn't keep track of all my activities. Which is no big deal, really, because *I* can barely keep track of them, and maybe I ought to just be grateful that he's not anything like Jordan. I mean, what Angela had to put *up* with.

Even if Jordan does have eyes as nice as Brad Pitt's, that's no reason for him to break up with her, just because she wouldn't have sex with him. Would Brad Pitt be so heartless?

I don't think so.

JORDAN

Wait a second. Isn't tonight New Year's Eve?

Two weeks later, the holiday break was over, and Angela woke up one morning with a start. Feeling breathless, she stared at the ceiling for a second, trying to figure out what day it was, and why she could possibly feel so good about it, whatever it was.

Then it hit her. Two things, actually. One: She'd just been having an erotic dream. Two: It hadn't featured Jordan. In any part. Not even as the towel boy who handed Corey Helfrick a towel at the gym. A towel that was made out of saltines. Or Triscuits, she couldn't tell which.

I loved Jordan Catalano so much and talked about him

so much and thought about him so much, it was like he was living inside me: like for a while he had taken possession of my soul. Angela smiled. *But now I'm over him!*

She threw the covers back and jumped out of bed. She wasn't possessed by anyone anymore. She was herself again.

She turned on the radio and started dancing around the room to one of her favorite songs by the Violent Femmes, the music blasting from the portable CD player on her dresser.

Fifteen minutes later, when she ate three huge slices of French toast for breakfast, her parents stared at her, speechless, as if she had dyed her hair again overnight— purple or blue this time. What could she say to explain?

I feel like Jordan has been surgically removed from my heart. And I'm free! Was she really supposed to tell them that? It was much better to keep something like that to yourself. It sounded too stupid or analytical or self-help-esque if you said things like that out loud.

But *she* knew.

"Wow. Abyssinia Churchill's auditioning?" Angela asked. She, Rayanne, and Rickie were standing in the back of the auditorium, checking out the auditions for *Our Town*. Rayanne wanted the lead role of Emily, and she'd spent half the night at Angela's house, rehearsing.

Angela was glad they were doing more stuff together again, now that she and Jordan were completely over. She'd felt guilty, as if she'd abandoned Rayanne.

"She's good," Rickie commented, watching Abyssinia.

"Yeah, she's really good. Screw this." Rayanne started to walk out, but Angela grabbed her arm.

"So? Don't let her psych you out—you're just as good," Angela told her.

Rayanne shook her head. "I can't believe I let you talk me into auditioning for this stupid play. *Our Town.* What is that, anyway?"

"Rayanne, you can do this. Just do what you did last night at my house!" She turned to Rickie. "You should have seen her. She, like...*became* Emily."

Rayanne smiled. "I became *you.* Emily's supposed to be sweet and innocent."

"So?" Angela scoffed.

"So I just imitated you!" Rayanne said.

"Wait a second, I think you might be next," Rickie said. "They're, like, almost at the G's."

"You really think I'm sweet and innocent?" Angela asked. For some reason, she couldn't think of anything more offensive. She wasn't either one of those, couldn't Rayanne see?

"You really thought I was good last night?" Rayanne asked, in her own world of stage fright.

"If you knew the dream I had about Corey Helfrick last night, you wouldn't think I was so sweet and innocent," Angela bragged.

"You had a dream about Corey? Like...a sex dream?" Rayanne asked.

"Join the club," Rickie muttered.

"Anyway, it proved another thing—I am *so* over Jordan Catalano."

"Yeah, yeah, yeah." Rayanne propped her foot on the arm of a chair and started tying her sneaker laces. "We've all heard that before."

"Well...this time it's for real. First of all, he was only my boyfriend, in the, like, technical sense, for about a minute. And second of all, I don't think we were ever right for each other. As friends, maybe. But that's it, it's over, and it is *such* a relief to have my life back."

"Rayanne Graff?" Mr. Katimski called into the auditorium.

"Oh my God…"

"Rayanne, think of it this way. Acting is sort of like lying, right? And who lies better than you?" Angela pointed out.

Rayanne stared at her for a second. "When something matters to you? You do this thing where you flick your hair? And you stand sort of off-balance, like this."

Angela shoved her toward the stage. "Quit studying me and get in there!" Rayanne walked down the aisle toward Mr. Katimski. "She *is* really good," Angela told Rickie.

"I'm sure she is," Rickie said. "I mean, of course. She's Rayanne."

The next morning, Angela pulled a sweater off the top shelf of her locker.

"I bet your pal Abyssinia will get the part. You must be so proud," Rayanne said.

"Shut up! I barely know her. She helped me with some geometry once, okay? Anyway, I'm proud of you. Your audition went great—"

"I didn't cry right," Rayanne interrupted, shaking her head. "I should have cried more how you cry. First you do these little sniffles, then your mouth sort of collapses on one side…" Rayanne sniffled, then twisted her mouth.

Rickie walked up and studied her for a second. "Why are you crying like Angela?"

Angela laughed, embarrassed. "Shut up, I don't cry like that!"

Rayanne suddenly stopped her phony sobbing and grabbed Angela's arm. "Corey Helfrick. Twelve o'clock."

"What?" Angela asked.

"Where?" Rickie added.

"Oh sure, Rayanne. And he's wearing a towel, right?" Angela joked. "See, in my dream he was wearing this really weird towel that was made, like, out of crackers, and it started to crumble—"

"Angela—" Rickie said in a warning voice.

She turned around. Corey was standing behind her. *Why do people have to constantly sneak up on me? It's like some sort of childhood game that I keep losing.*

"Hi," Corey said.

"Hi," the three of them replied in unison.

"Nice cry," Corey said. "Your audition, I mean."

"You saw it? You're in the Drama Club?" Angela asked.

"He paints scenery," Rickie said. He pressed his lips together. "I mean…right?"

Corey nodded.

"So Corey. Forget painting," Rayanne said, giggling. "We were just having this discussion. Maybe you can help. When you eat soup, what type of cracker do you have with it?"

"Quit it!" Angela pretended to punch Rayanne. *How much more embarrassing does it get than to see the person you actually dreamed about…by your locker, like, in broad daylight?*

"Rickie, I have to talk to you." Rayanne pulled him aside and they immediately started having a private conversation by the window across the hallway.

Angela looked at Corey. Over his shoulder, she could just make out Jordan's loping figure, coming down the hall toward them. "So, what's the scenery going to be like?" she asked Corey.

"You really want to know?" Corey seemed surprised.

"Yeah, of course." Angela checked to see whether Jordan was within voice range yet. He was looking right at her. "I mean, is it going to be realistic-looking or..."

"It's supposed to be sort of artificial, actually," Corey said. "See, when the play was first produced..." Corey started to explain the history of Thornton Wilder's *Our Town*.

This is nothing like my dream, Angela thought. She could see that Jordan was watching the two of them, though, so she smiled as brightly as she could. *I like Corey. I do. I mean, I had a dream about this person, so I'm attracted to him. And I want to pay this much attention to everything he says. It's not just because Jordan is watching.*

"I didn't know you were interested in art," Corey finished.

"I don't know that much, but I'm interested, definitely. And I would love to help! *Definitely!*" Angela said loudly, feeling like a cartoon character with all-capital blurbs above her head. SCREECH! HELP! LOOK AT ME!

"You'd love to what?" Corey looked a little confused.

"Help with the scenery sometime," Angela said, still grinning unnaturally widely.

"Okay, well, I'll let you know when we need help," Corey said with a shrug.

"Great!" Angela waved at Corey, and hurried off down the hall to her next class. *It's kind of weird, going to all my classes again. I feel like I might actually be learning something.* For a minute she felt strangely guilty about having just used Corey that way. But maybe she really was interested; maybe she'd help paint scenery after all. Maybe Jordan *didn't* still influence everything she did.

I am over him, she told herself. *I am. I just...slipped up, a little. Like, off the wagon or whatever. One of the wheels broke. But I'm back on.*

Angela was at her locker the next morning, digging through her backpack, when Brian came down the hallway, his camera slung around his neck. She smiled at him, but when he saw her, he looked away, almost as if he were afraid of her. He walked right past her.

He must have the flu or something, Angela thought. The last time Brian Krakow had ignored her in the hallway had been right after their measles shots in the first grade, and right *before* he passed out cold on the linoleum floor. In her opinion, Brian was always noticing her *too* much. Taking a break for one day might be a good idea.

She closed her locker and was about to head for homeroom when she saw Rayanne walking at the end of the hallway. "Rayanne!" she called. "Did you get the part?"

Rayanne turned the corner and disappeared without answering.

Angela just stood there, confused. *Why doesn't anyone want to talk to me?*

And then she started to get this odd feeling. The same kind of feeling she had once when her grandfather was sick, and her parents weren't telling her. There were all these weird conversations late at night that no one ever mentioned. It was the same kind of feeling she had when she caught her father talking to that woman when she came home from Let's Bolt. Like...awful things were happening all around her, and they didn't *exactly* involve her. But they did. Only everyone was trying to keep something from her, like she was too innocent or naive to find out.

Couldn't they see that she wasn't? That she'd been through more than enough, and she knew life wasn't the way she'd always pictured it? Why couldn't somebody just *tell* her? What was wrong?

She turned to walk upstairs and almost bumped right into Corey. "Oh, sorry!" he said. "Hi."

"Hi," Angela said with a nervous laugh. "Sorry."

"You know, there's something I need to tell you," Corey said. He hesitated.

Angela felt like she was going to shake him by the neck. *Just tell me! Do I have toilet paper stuck to my heel or what?*

"Hi!" Rickie said, coming up behind Angela.

"Hi. So...what did you want to tell me?" Angela prompted Corey.

"Oh!" Corey took a deep breath. "Just that we're painting the oak tree today after school, and we could use a few more people, if you're not busy."

"That sounds great," Rickie said enthusiastically. "I mean, I think I have some free time. Don't you?" he asked Angela.

"Yeah, let's do it," she said, shrugging. So there wasn't anything anyone wanted to tell her. She was just imagining the whole thing.

"Angela?" Sharon walked into their empty science classroom later that afternoon, a few minutes before class started. Angela was already at her desk, finishing a lab report that was due.

"Hey," Angela said, glancing at Sharon.

Sharon sat down beside her, at Brian's desk. "I have something to, like...something really hard to say to somebody and I don't know how."

"Really?" Angela pressed her pen firmly against the page, making sure she'd have a clear carbon copy in her lab notebook. "What? Are you going to tell Kyle you're, like, leaving him for Brad Pitt?" She laughed.

"No." Sharon sounded uncertain. "Angela? Look at me."

Angela glanced up. Sharon's mouth was scrunched together, the way it got when she felt carsick. "What's the big deal?" Angela asked.

"I asked Brian Krakow to make a videotape for yearbook, okay? And I *told* him to go to Pike Street, to get some candids or whatever," Sharon explained. "So he was there, last night. And he got something on tape. A candid. And you should know."

"Know *what*?" Angela said. "I'm not on yearbook, okay? I don't care what kind of video—"

"Rayanne and Jordan were there," Sharon interrupted. "Together. I mean, they left together. And they, like...got into his car. And—"

"So Jordan gave her a ride home," Angela said. "Big deal. I mean, I'm *so* shocked."

"No, Angela," Sharon pleaded. "They were kissing. She was drunk. He was too. They didn't know what they were doing. They, like...had sex."

"Oh my God! Do you expect me to, like, believe you?" Angela said. "Rayanne and Jordan—and Brian just happened to capture this on *film*?"

Sharon nodded. "Pretty much. I know, it's terrible. But Rayanne was drinking and—"

"Do you expect me to think that you would, like...defend her if this was true? Which it isn't." Angela laughed, but her laugh sounded hollow and shrill, even to herself, as if she had forced it out of a hiding place.

"Angela, ask Brian if you want," Sharon said, standing up. "But I just thought you should know. Rayanne's, like, *so* not your friend."

In a daze, Angela watched Sharon take a seat diagonally across the aisle from her. Jordan and Rayanne? But they'd never do something like that to her. It was impossible. It would be breaking every rule known to humanity. It would be...inhuman.

"Rickie, you would not believe—" Corey handed Angela a paintbrush when she walked into the auditorium after science class. "Oh, thanks!" she told him.

"Make sure you wipe it off before you change colors, okay?"

"I will!" Angela grinned, feeling a little out of control, as if she might burst into tears or hysterical laughter, depending on what Rickie said. "So, you would not believe what Sharon told me," she whispered frantically.

Rickie painted the tree trunk without looking at her. "What?"

Angela laughed. "Oh, this is so unreal. Like, how Rayanne supposedly did it. With Jordan. And how Brian filmed it and now he has it on video." She shook her head, dipping the brush into a can of brownish paint. "I thought Sharon was *over* this jealousy about Rayanne, I mean, we've sort of been friends again for a while. But obviously she isn't over it. Or else why would she tell me something as hateful as that?" She watched Rickie's face carefully.

He slowly turned around, facing her. "Because it's true."

Chapter 14

Brian leaped off the bed, where he'd been lying half-dressed, listening to his Walkman. "What are you doing here?" He grabbed a T-shirt off the back of his desk chair and yanked it over his head. "You know, people should tell people they have visitors!" he yelled to his parents, his voice disappearing into a cotton-polyester blend.

"I need that videotape," Angela demanded.

"Huh?" Brian's head popped out of the shirt, his curly hair standing on end with static.

"The videotape. Come on, Brian, just give it to me," Angela insisted. "I want to see it. I have a right to see it."

"Excuse me, but I, like, returned that sex tape with your backpack a long time ago," Brian said, shoving some stuff under his bed.

"Not that tape. The other tape," Angela said.

"What are you talking about?"

"Don't pretend you don't know what I'm talking about! This is partly your fault!" Angela cried.

"My...*what*? This is my fault? *My* fault? How?" Brian asked.

"Just give me the tape!" She looked around the room anxiously.

"For-forget it!" Brian stammered. "I have other things on it, okay?"

"I don't care!" Angela said. Suddenly, she spotted Brian's video camera, the one he used for yearbook, on his desk. She made a move for it. So did Brian. She grabbed it first and, popping it open, pulled out the cassette.

"Don't watch it. I mean, I don't think you really want to...see it. It'll just make you feel worse," Brian said quietly.

Angela stared at the tape. There it was.

Her proof.

She dropped the tape onto the floor and ran out of his room.

"Angela?"

The door to the girls' room opened and closed. Angela hovered in her stall, deciding whether or not to go out.

"Angela, I know you're in here," Rickie said. "And you can't stay in here forever."

Angela lifted the half-broken metal latch and walked out of the stall. "Rickie, I'm sorry, but...I have to be alone."

"You've, like, been alone. For days."

"I need years," Angela said. "Rickie, I still can't believe it!"

Rickie nodded, taking a step toward her. "I know."

"To just do that? Behind my back? I mean, who do

they think they are?" Angela threw up her hands. She was so sick of thinking about it, of picturing it. She hadn't even talked about it with anyone yet. Who was she supposed to talk to? She felt completely humiliated by everyone. They'd either been involved, or they *knew*. Before her. Which was almost unforgivable, even if it wasn't their fault.

"I know," Rickie said. "Actually? I don't know."

"I could kill them," Angela said fiercely. "Both of them. Like, with my bare hands."

"I know. I mean, I could almost, so I can imagine...but you do have to leave this room. Eventually."

"I can't," Angela said. "I can't, like...go out there, and run into her. Or him. Or—God!—him *and* her, together." She felt like she was about to throw up. Which was another reason to stay in the bathroom all day; it was more convenient.

"Well, don't worry about that. I mean, they're completely avoiding each other." Rickie shrugged.

"Really?" Angela asked. Why did that give her hope? For what? What good thing could possibly happen now?

"Angela, look." Rickie took her hands, clasping them tightly. "You *can't let* their stupid actions control your life. You've gotta, like...lead your own life, and forget about them."

Angela stared at the graffiti on the wall. She'd almost memorized it over the past few days. That was kind of pathetic. "You're right. And you know what? Two can play at this game."

"Game?" Rickie repeated.

"They both think I'm some innocent little girl? Who they can treat as badly as they want, because I don't know any better? Well, they're wrong. I'll *show* them how wrong." She smiled grimly at Rickie. "Thanks."

"You're welcome. I guess."

Angela strode out of the girls' room, head held high. Down the hallway, she saw a cluster of students, looking at something on the wall. *It's either a giant cockroach…or the* Our Town *cast list,* she thought.

Then she saw Rayanne, hopping up and down in the group, trying to get a glimpse of the list. Angela's heart felt like it had just been ripped open all over again.

The hallway is such a dangerous place. They check us for firearms when we come in every morning. But that doesn't help. Because the things that really hurt? Can't be identified by, like…a metal detector. They're too far inside.

Two boys went past Angela, complaining about how they hadn't gotten parts. *I hope she doesn't get one either,* Angela thought bitterly. *Not even as an extra.* She kept walking toward her science classroom, which was a few doors up from the bulletin board.

Then she heard the shriek. Rayanne's shriek. And saw her jumping up and down in the hall, like a Super Ball somebody had just bounced. "Hey, Angela!" she called.

She got the part, and she wants to tell me. As if I'd be happy for her. As if I'd want to know anything about her life, ever again.

Ignoring her, Angela walked into her class and slumped into her seat next to Brian. He gave her a concerned look, and she just smiled. *Don't feel sorry for me,* she thought. *The last thing I need right now is Brian Krakow pitying me.*

I was only the best friend she could ever have. And she…did it. With Jordan. And she knew how it would make me feel. And she did it anyway. And enjoyed it, probably. They both did.

I am such a fool.

No. I was such a fool. She sat up straighter in her seat. *Not anymore.*

After class, Angela scanned the cast list on the bulletin board. There it was:

EMILY.............................RAYANNE GRAFF

It was like seeing some horrible dictator get an award for good citizenship. Like some really dopey sitcom winning an Emmy while your favorite new show got canceled.

"Angela!"

She turned away from the board and started walking away. When would people stop calling her name? No wonder she'd been hiding in the girls' room. *I want them to both stop trying to make it up to me. Because they can't.*

"Hey, didn't you hear me?" Jordan was tagging along at her elbow.

"No," Angela retorted. She stopped walking and faced him. She had a morbid curiosity to find out what he would say, how he thought he could possibly explain sleeping with her best friend. Did he think there were *words*?

"Here." He took a pen out of the pocket of his vintage gas station shirt and handed it to her.

Angela stared at the pen as he placed it between her fingers. "Why are you giving me this?"

"Because. It's yours," Jordan said.

Angela held it out toward him. "I don't want it."

"Well, it's your pen," Jordan argued.

"So?" Angela cried.

"So, you lent it to me in Katimski's, remember?"

Angela stared at the floor. She would not look at him; she didn't want to take the chance. She felt strong, but not superhuman. "Not really." *In fact, I'm trying to forget. You. Me. Everything.*

"Okay." Jordan sighed. "So, if it's not yours, then, like...give it back."

Angela thought about it for a second. Why should she give Jordan anything—especially of hers? "No," she said.

She peeked up at him through the hair hanging in front of her face. He was looking at her the same way he had that night they'd officially broken up, at her house. The way that made her heart start to creak open, like a rusty hinge.

Suddenly Angela headed straight for the trash can by the water fountain and tossed the pen into it, enjoying the neat metal clang it made as it banged into the side.

"Hello!" Angela said brightly, walking into the backstage area where she, Rickie, and Corey were painting backdrop screens.

"Hi. Grab a brush," Corey said.

"Sure. In a second. Could I, like...talk to you first?" Angela asked.

"Are you okay?" Rickie was just staring at her, the way Sharon had when Angela dyed her hair, as if she had completely lost her mind.

Okay, so maybe she had changed a couple of things about her appearance—like she was wearing double-action jet black mascara, and she'd braided a piece of her hair, and she was wearing Fire Red lipstick instead of her usual Pale Peach Frost. *What, am I only allowed to change once a year? Like I'm a tree?* "Yeah, I'm fine," Angela said. Corey put his brush down and followed her into the hall. "So, do you have anything to drink?" she asked.

Corey looked surprised. "You drink? Really?"

"Why not? Why shouldn't I?" Angela argued.

"I don't know." Corey shrugged.

"What, I'm too *innocent* or something? Well, I'm sick of being like that!" she declared. *What am I even doing? This is not me*, Angela thought, right before she started kissing Corey.

He pulled back, wiping the lipstick off his mouth. "Angela?"

"What?"

"Look, um, it's just..."

"What's wrong with me? Is there something wrong with me?"

"No! Look, let's just go back to—"

"Oh God, can't we just get out of here and get really drunk or something?"

"What the hell are you talking about? You don't drink."

Angela whirled around and saw Rayanne. "Get away from me."

"Excuse us, Corey," Rayanne said. Corey disappeared in two seconds, running back into the auditorium. Angela started to follow him. She didn't want to be left alone with Rayanne.

"You know, I never would have got the part if it wasn't for you," Rayanne said, chasing after her.

Angela kept walking.

"Go ahead if you want to. I mean, do it!" Rayanne said excitedly. "Get really loaded, and destroy everything that matters to you. Then you'll know what it's like."

"Look. I don't care anymore. Just go away," Angela said.

"No," said Rayanne, grabbing Angela's arm. "You're not the only one who got hurt."

"Oh, really. Well, forgive me if I can't feel your *pain*, Rayanne!" Angela cried, finally facing her.

"You didn't lose anything," Rayanne went on. "You lost...a terrible, selfish friend. A guy you never really had. You lost nothing."

Angela stared at Rayanne. *If I lost nothing, then why do I feel so rotten?* She was so angry and upset, she couldn't even speak. Not even to yell at Rayanne, the way she'd fantasized about.

"I lost a really good friend. I lost everything," Rayanne said.

Angela swallowed, struck by Rayanne's honesty. Then Rickie was suddenly standing there, and Angela looked at him as if he were a life preserver somebody had flung to her in the ocean. She'd almost broken down. She'd almost made up with Rayanne.

Rayanne looked at Rickie a moment, then she turned and walked through the door to the auditorium.

"I'm glad she got that part," Rickie said.

"What?" Angela cried. "Whose side are you on?"

"I'm on your side. It's, like, impossible to be on Rayanne's side," Rickie said. "Even though I kind of understand it."

"What do you mean?"

"Well, face it. She's always kind of wanted to *be* you. Ever since she met you. And in a way? I think that for that one night...she was, like, pretending she *was* you," Rickie said. "And maybe he was doing that too. In a way.

Pretending, maybe, that he was with you."

Sometimes Rickie is, like...too profound. I want to believe him, but he always sees the best in a situation.

"I'm on your side," he continued. "There's no question. But can I ask you something?"

"Sure," Angela said.

"Why are you suddenly making this big play for Corey? When you already know how I feel about him?"

"Because! You told me you were over him!" Angela said.

"But guess how I felt," Rickie said. "When you started going after him."

Angela looked at him. "I don't have to guess. I'm sorry. I wasn't...thinking." *Like, about anyone, besides myself.* It was the same thing: She'd told Rayanne she was *over* Jordan, so...

No, it wasn't the same thing, she decided. Because Rayanne *knew* she was still in love with Jordan. Even though Angela said she wasn't. *And good friends? That's their, like...job. To know you better than you know yourself. So they can stop you. From going after boys you're not interested in. From drinking when you're not supposed to anymore...*

But it didn't matter now. There were some things that couldn't be taken back. Like when you had a library book out too long, and you couldn't find it anywhere, and they made you buy it. And even if you found it? It was too late. Your mistake. You, like...owned the book now, and you didn't want it.

"Wait a second. What—what happened to Chee Kwan?" Mr. Katimski asked in the middle of rehearsal.

Angela, Rickie, and Corey were carrying a flat onto

the back of the stage to work on.

"She left," Abyssinia said. "Curfew, I guess."

"Well...who's back there? Angela!" Mr. Katimski called. "You want to come up here a minute and read Chee's part?"

Angela froze. "Not really," she murmured.

"Come on, it's just a stupid play and we need a girl. Get up here!"

Angela looked at Rickie, who shrugged. Then she hurried downstage. "Just look on with Abyssinia," Mr. Katimski instructed her. Angela walked past Rayanne and stood beside Abyssinia.

"And, uh, Rayanne?" Mr. Katimski continued. "Would you kindly take three steps downstage, and could you...stop acting? Please?"

"What?" Rayanne asked.

"Stop acting. There's really no need," Mr. Katimski explained. "Your character, Emily, is dead, and only now is she realizing that every moment of her life was precious. And that she never appreciated what she had when she had it. Just imagine, Rayanne, what that would feel like."

Rayanne stared down at the stage for a moment. She closed her eyes, then began the scene. "I can't go on. It goes so fast. We don't have time to look at one another." Then, looking up, she turned slightly toward Angela. "I didn't realize. So all that was going on, and we never noticed..."

Angela couldn't stand to look at Rayanne. She wasn't acting at all. She was saying the lines, but she was talking about *them*, about *their* lives. Angela bit her lip and clutched the edge of the script that Abyssinia was holding.

"Take me back up the hill to my grave. But first, wait. One more look…Good-bye. Good-bye, world! Good-bye, Grovers Corners—Mama and Papa. Good-bye to clocks ticking…"

It was too much for Angela to take. This speech, which reminded her of all the good times they'd had together: her and Rickie and Rayanne in the girls' room, laughing when Rickie'd said good-bye to everything.…her and Jordan in the boiler room, after the note he'd sent her, spelling her name wrong. It was all wonderful. And it was all terrible. Because none of it would ever happen again. A tear ran down Angela's cheek.

"Do any human beings ever realize life while they live it? Every, every minute?" Rayanne asked quietly.

"No," Abyssinia said, her voice startling Angela. "Saints and poets maybe, they do some."

"I'm ready to go back," Rayanne announced.

There was silence on the stage. Then Abyssinia gently nudged Angela's arm, and she realized everyone was waiting for her to speak her lines.

She swallowed and brushed at her wet cheek. "Were you happy?" Her voice sounded small and inconsequential to her.

"No," Rayanne said. She turned and looked straight at Angela. For the first time, Angela could see that she was crying. And this time she didn't look like Emily—or Angela—crying. She looked like Rayanne. "I should have listened to you. That's all human beings are. Just blind people."

Angela looked at Rayanne through tear-blurred eyes. It was all starting to sink in, with a kind of finality and understanding she hadn't felt a few days—even a few hours—before. Her so-called best friend had actually slept with her so-called boyfriend. Together, Rayanne and Jordan had betrayed her, and they had been the most important people to her...

And now they were out of her life.

But maybe they didn't have to be...at least not permanently.

Rayanne's words echoed in her head. Her voice seemed small, quiet...apologetic. *"That's all human beings are. Just blind people."*

Maybe Rickie was right, Angela thought. Maybe Rayanne and Jordan were both searching for a part of Angela in each other. Or searching for something they didn't understand, and couldn't see.

To Angela, they'd always seemed older and more knowledgeable about things. But the truth was, they hadn't known what they were doing any more than she'd known.

But now, at this moment, I do know a few things. About friendship, and betrayal.

And maybe about forgiveness.

Angela looked up at Rayanne. For the first time in days, Angela risked a small smile at her friend...a connection. Rayanne nodded. Her cheeks were wet, her eyes shining. She smiled back.

And I know something else, thought Angela. *What really matters in my so-called life...is going to be up to me.*

After she got home from rehearsal, Angela dropped her backpack just inside the front door, then went back outside. Brian was riding his bike down the sidewalk on the other side of the street, toward her. She started to cross the street, and he leaped off the sidewalk on his bike and loudly skidded to a stop in front of her.

Angela rolled her eyes. "Like I'm impressed, Krakow."

"Like I am," Brian replied.

"Look, can I...I know I'm constantly asking you for stuff, but could I just maybe borrow your bike for, like, half an hour?"

"Where are you going?"

"I don't know," Angela said.

"What do you mean? You don't *know* know, or you don't want to *say* but you know?" Brian said.

"Just give me the bike, okay?" Angela asked. "I want to go for a ride."

"This doesn't involve Jordan Catalano in any way, does it?" Brian asked.

Angela just held out her hand and waited for the inevitable. Finally, Brian got off his bike and pushed it toward her. "I need it back this time. Like, the same *day*."

"You'll get it back," Angela promised. She climbed onto the banana seat and took off down the street, on a route she used to take when she rode to junior high every day. She rode quietly for a long time, just breathing the fresh, cold, winter air and thinking.

She turned right and headed over a railroad bridge. As she pedaled up a steep hill, she thought about everything that had happened to her so far this year. Much of it hadn't been easy; but, all in all, it seemed—in her humble opinion—that her so-called life was finally...beginning.

When she reached the top of the hill, she lifted her hands off the handlebars. Wavering back and forth, she began to coast down the hill.

She was smiling. Then laughing.

She might crash, but probably she wouldn't. She'd have to watch how wide she took the turn at the bottom.

And I'll have to remember that it's still possible to feel this good. About myself. No matter what happens.

At the bottom of the hill, Angela tightly gripped the handlebars and turned the corner. A little faster than she used to, maybe, but not out of control.

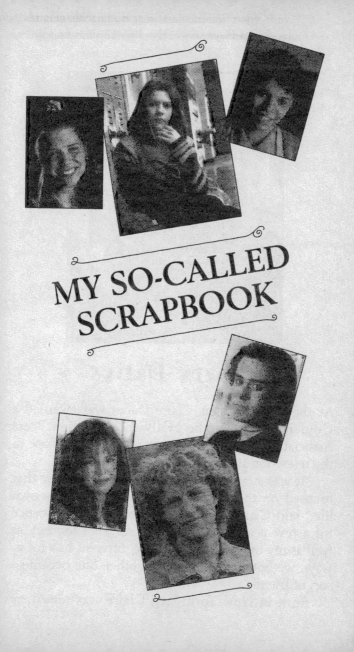

MY SO-CALLED
SCRAPBOOK

Claire Danes

At the age of fifteen, Claire Danes was awarded a Golden Globe by the Hollywood Foreign Press Association for her performance as Angela Chase in the television series *My So-Called Life*.

"It was strange and wonderful to do a show that focused on things that were going on in my own life," said Claire. "I lived a rather dual adolescence for a few years, going through Angela's journey as well as my own. Although we're different in a lot of ways, we both influenced each other. She became a sort of friend."

Born in New York City, Claire was raised by

artistic parents in the New York neighborhood of SoHo, an area full of art galleries and crowded cafes. Claire knew from an early age that she wanted to be a performer. "When I was five," said Claire, "I remember my parents got a video camera and that weekend I just exploded."

She started dance class at the age of six and began her acting lessons a few years later. At the age of ten she enrolled at the Lee Strasberg Theatre Institute, and by sixth grade she was attending the Professional Performing Arts School, where she studied drama two hours a day. By the time she reached the age of eleven, Claire had performed in an off-off Broadway play, a few short films, and a small feature film.

"I got hooked," said Claire of acting.

After a week of auditions in Los Angeles, she landed the lead in *My So-Called Life*. As Marshall Herskovitz, one of the executive producers, explained, "If we hadn't found Claire, we would have waited to do the series. She was the linchpin."

These days, Claire is remaining busy with acting roles. She recently received rave reviews for her role as Beth in the feature-film version of Louisa May Alcott's *Little Women*. Claire's upcoming films include a role in *How to Make an American Quilt*, opposite Winona Ryder; she will also appear in Jodie Foster's *Home for the Holidays*, opposite Holly Hunter.

Besides acting, Claire enjoys both dance and gymnastics.

Jared Leto

Within a year of moving to Los Angeles, Jared Leto landed the role of Jordan, the cool, quiet object of Angela Chase's affection on *My So-Called Life*, the show produced by the creators of the television drama *thirtysomething*. Never having seen *thirtysomething*, Jared was unaware of the style of its directors or the impact of its content—until he saw his own pilot for *My So-Called Life*, directed by Scott Winant. "It blew me away," said the actor.

He had moved to Los Angeles from New York in March 1992, leaving behind his filmmaking studies at the School of Visual Arts to pursue an acting career. Without a headshot or résumé, armed only with his own motivation and nerve, Jared landed an agent within a week of his arrival. Anxious to work on quality projects, he passed on a few before winning the role of Jordan.

Jared's determination can be traced to his upbringing by his mother, who encouraged him and his brother to be involved in the arts. Born on a bayou in Louisiana, Jared traveled extensively as a child, living in such diverse locations as Haiti and in a commune in Colorado. "My mom's father was in the air force, so moving around a lot was a normal way of life," said Jared.

Driven from a young age, he took a job at twelve years old washing dishes at the 3 Pigs Barbecue in Virginia. "That was the place to work," offered the actor. "It's where all the stoners hung out, and to have a job there—even at $2.50 an hour with taxes taken out—was a trip." Always enterprising, Jared became a doorman at age sixteen, with the help of a fake I.D. Ultimately, he enrolled at the University of Arts in Philadelphia to study painting before transferring to the School of Visual Arts in New York.

Jared will soon begin production on his first feature film, *How to Make an American Quilt*, opposite Winona Ryder and Dermot Mulroney. He also recently starred in *The Cool & the Crazy*, an original Showtime movie.

Of his work on *My So-Called Life*, Jared explained that, as with any acting job, there were challenging and rewarding aspects. "The biggest challenge was learning to *not always* make the moments a huge deal, to sometimes just live and breathe and talk as the character. And the most rewarding thing was to be a part of something that was good, honest, and had quality. There's no better way to start a career."

A. J. Langer

As the fast-lane friend of Angela in *My So-Called Life*, A. J. brought both brash and fun-loving elements to her role as Rayanne Graff. But A. J. herself is nothing like the role she plays.

"Rayanne is *very* different from me," said A. J. "Making her 100 percent was the biggest challenge for me. All the little things that seemed so spontaneous—they weren't spontaneous to me, so they took a little work. But, then again, it's the greatest challenge you could ever imagine. It's the actor's dream to play your opposite."

A. J. was born in Columbus, Ohio, and moved with her family to Los Angeles when she was five years old. It was a high school algebra teacher who got A. J. her first big break. During a chance viewing of A. J. in action on the high school speech team, the teacher gave A. J. the idea of acting as a profession. The teacher had connections to an agent, and A. J. was soon on her way to auditions and making acting her career.

My So-Called Life was A. J.'s second regular role in a television series. Her first was in *Drexell's Class*, starring Dabney Coleman.

A. J.'s additional television appearances include guest-starring parts in *The Wonder Years, Hangin' with Mr. Cooper, In the Heat of the Night, Blossom,*

Beverly Hills 90210, *Baywatch*, and *Parker Lewis Can't Lose*. She has also appeared in the feature films *The People Under the Stairs* and *And You Thought Your Parents Were Weird*.

Wilson Cruz

In what was a first for a series regular, Wilson Cruz portrayed a teenager searching for his true sexual identity and for life's—and love's—deeper meaning in *My So-Called Life.*

Wilson brought sensitivity and intelligence to the role, and said of his experience on the series: "I am so proud to have played Rickie Vasquez. To me he is a beacon of light in a world darkened by ignorance and intolerance."

Born in New York City, Wilson moved with his family to San Bernadino, California, where he currently lives.

His acting experience includes both television and theatre. Prior to his role on *My So-Called Life*, Wilson was a series regular in the television show *Great Scott.*

Wilson's theatrical experience includes performing with Young Americans and roles in *Cradle of Fire, Supporting Cast, Becoming Memories, Roar of the Greasepaint...*, and *Wedding Band.*

Devon Gummersall

As the brainy Brian Krakow in *My So-Called Life*, Devon Gummersall brought humor and depth to his portrayal of Angela Chase's peculiarly perceptive neighbor. Said the equally perceptive Devon of his work in the series: "Brian Krakow was a character that was constantly a challenge and a joy to play. He was a diamond in the rough, the kind of person who could change the world...just not in high school."

Born in Durango, Colorado, Devon moved to Los Angeles with his father, an artist. Devon explained that his initial interest in acting was enhanced by being around his father's artistic community.

Devon's first acting experience actually came with an appearance in a Stouffer's commercial. He went on to land roles in both television and films. His feature-film credits include roles in *My Girl II* and *Beethoven's 2nd*.

His other television-series credits include guest-starring parts in *Almost Home*, *Step by Step*, *Peaceable Kingdom*, *Dream On*, and *Blossom*.

In addition to his proficiency in a wealth of sports, including in-line skating, tennis, swimming, basketball, and baseball, Devon enjoys writing—especially poetry.

Devon Odessa

Born in Parkersburg, Virginia, Devon Odessa first gained an interest in acting when she and her family moved to New Orleans. There she appeared in a production of *Cat on a Hot Tin Roof*. Later Devon moved to Los Angeles with her mother, who is also an actress.

Fans of *My So-Called Life* recognize Devon for the energy and style she brought to the role of Sharon Cherski, the friend Angela dumps because of her too-good image. Devon said that from the start she felt drawn to the role.

Although Devon initially read for the parts of both Angela Chase and Rayanne Graff, she consistently asked the casting director if she could read for the part of Sharon Cherski, because she felt connected with that character.

"What I loved about playing the character of Sharon," said Devon, "was that Winnie [Holzman, the series creator] cut through all the stereotype and allowed me to explore darker, more complex issues that bubble underneath a character that could outwardly be perceived as the goody-two-shoes perk monster in total control. It's easy to slot people and dismiss them after a first impression, and I hope the role of Sharon has encouraged people to take the

time to look beyond the facade, and appreciate that everyone has issues, and nobody is perfect and has everything they want.

"We are all connected in a very fundamental way," added Devon, "which is why *My So-Called Life* was so important to so many people. We all shared, and came out the better for it."

Devon's other television acting credits include recurring roles in CBS's *Angel Falls*. She has also appeared as a guest star in episodes of *The Wonder Years*, *Full House*, *Step by Step*, *Highway to Heaven*, *Hunter*, *The Facts of Life*, and *My Talk Show*. Her made-for-television movies include *Girl of the Limberlost* and *Extreme Close-Up*.

Her feature films include MGM's *Pumpkinhead*.

Devon is a graduate of Notre Dame High School in Sherman Oaks, California. She enjoys dancing, horseback riding, tennis, and skating.

BESS ARMSTRONG created the role of Angela's mother, Patty Chase, in *My So-Called Life.* Born in Ruxton, Maryland, Bess began acting at the age of five. She had an agreement with her parents that she could act in plays so long as she remained on the honor roll. She kept her bargain. An honors graduate of Bryn Mawr School for Girls, Bess went on to earn degrees in Latin and theatre from Brown University. She has worked in both television and in films. Her first feature film was Alan Alda's *The Four Seasons.* Her other film roles included *High Road to China, Nothing in Common, The Skateboard Kid,* and *Dream Lover.* Bess and her husband have two sons and live in Los Angeles.

TOM IRWIN portrayed Graham Chase, Angela's well-meaning but sometimes weary father. Tom is a native of Peoria, Illinois, and a graduate of Illinois State University, where he first became interested in acting. His career began with the prestigious Steppenwolf Theatre Company in Chicago. While there, he gained a wealth of experience in many productions, including the plays *Love Letters, The Homecoming, Cat on a Hot Tin Roof,* and *The Miss Firecracker Contest.* Tom has gone on to direct theatre and perform in television and film. His film credits include roles in *Mr. Jones, Deceived, Midnight Run, Light of Day,* and *Men Don't Leave.* Tom lives in both Chicago and Los Angeles with two cats named Michael Jordan and Frances Glass.

LISA WILHOIT portrayed Angela's ten-year-old little sister. Born in Los Angeles, Lisa is an accomplished gymnast who was used for stunt work in the feature film *Hook,* starring Robin Williams. Her additional feature film credits include voice-over work for *Addams Family Values, Dennis the Menace, Home Alone 2, Fearless, Searching for Bobby Fischer,* and *Wrestling Ernest Hemingway.* In television, Lisa was featured in the Hallmark Hall of Fame production *Talking with T. J.*

WINNIE HOLZMAN was the creator and co-executive producer of the critically acclaimed one-hour drama *My So-Called Life*. Winnie graduated from Princeton University, where she majored in English with a concentration in creative writing. After college, she studied acting at the Circle in the Square Theatre School in New York City. She then received a full scholarship to join the newly formed N.Y.U. Musical Theatre Program, where she met David Evans. Together they have written *Maggie and the Pirate*, a musical for children, *Back to Back*, a contemporary one-act opera, and *Birds of Paradise*, which was produced off-Broadway in 1987 and directed by Arthur Laurents.

Winnie met Marshall Herskovitz and Ed Zwick, the executive producers of the hit television series *thirtysomething*, in 1989. She was welcomed to join their writing staff after submitting a script. In her two seasons with *thirtysomething* she wrote nine episodes and received a Writer's Guild of America nomination. Her first feature film, a romantic comedy entitled *Till There Was You*, is slated for production this summer.

CATHERINE CLARK, the author of the novel based on *My So-Called Life*, grew up in western Massachusetts and now lives in Madison, Wisconsin. Catherine is a graduate of Wesleyan University, and she earned an M.F.A. in creative writing from Colorado State University. She has written several novels for children and young adults, including *What's So Funny About Ninth Grade?*, *Girl of the Year*, and *The Day I Met Him*. Also a writer of adult fiction, Catherine is currently working on a collection of short stories.

MARSHALL HERSKOVITZ, an executive producer of *My So-Called Life*, hails from Philadelphia and attended Brandeis University. After earning a master's degree in fine arts from the American Film Institute, Marshall went on to write and direct for a number of acclaimed television hits, including *Family*. With Ed Zwick, he created *thirtysomething*, an Emmy award-winning series. For his work, Marshall garnered many awards, including two Emmys, a Golden Globe, and two Director's Guild of America awards. In feature films, Marshall directed the Twentieth Century Fox release *Jack the Bear*, starring Danny DeVito. With Ed Zwick, Marshall has formed the Bedford Falls Company as the home of their future film and television projects.

ED ZWICK, an executive producer of *My So-Called Life*, is a native of Winnetka, Illinois. He began directing and acting in high school and trained as an apprentice at the Academy Festival in Lake Forest, Illinois. He graduated from Harvard and received a Rockefeller Fellowship to study theatre abroad. While in Paris, he worked for Woody Allen on the film *Love and Death*. Ed met Marshall Herkovitz while studying at the American Film Institute. He has amassed multiple awards for his work including three Emmys, the Humanitas prize, a Writer's Guild of America award, two Peabody awards, and a Director's Guild of America award. His feature-film directing career includes *About Last Night*, the Oscar-winning *Glory*, and *Legends of the Fall*, starring Sharon Cherski's favorite actor, Brad Pitt.

SCOTT WINANT, a co-executive producer and director of *My So-Called Life*, was born in New York City and earned a degree in cinema production from the University of Southern California. He started in the entertainment industry as a page for CBS-TV. He then served as a production assistant in television and films. With that experience, he began to produce and direct industrial and documentary films, and also worked on various projects as a film editor, cameraman, and special-effects coordinator. Scott was instrumental in establishing *thirtysomething*'s unique style of cinematic storytelling, which earned him numerous awards, including an Emmy for best directing. His other awards include a Golden Globe, a Peabody, and the Television Critics' Association award.

ZODIAC CHILLERS

It's written in the stars...
astro-fans are in for a thrill!

You can send in this coupon (with check or money order)
and have these books mailed directly to you!

☐ #1 **RAGE OF AQUARIUS** (0-679-87304-X) $3.99
   by Carol Ellis

☐ #2 **THE SCORPIO SOCIETY** (0-679-87305-8) $3.99
   by Carol Ellis

☐ #3 **IN LEO'S LAIR** (0-679-87306-6) $3.99
   by Carol Ellis

☐ #4 **TWISTED TAURUS** (0-679-87307-4) $3.99
   by Ellen Steiber

☐ #5 **NEVER LOVE A LIBRA** (0-679-87308-2) $3.99
   by Vicki Kamida

☐ #6 **PISCES DROWNING** (0-679-87309-0) $3.99
   by Ellen Steiber

Subtotal . . . . $ ____
Shipping and handling. . . . . $ 3.00
Sales tax (where applicable) . . . . $ ____
Total amount enclosed. . . . . $ ____

Name _____

Address _____

City _____ State _____ Zip _____

Make your check or money order (no cash or C.O.D.s) payable to Random House
and mail to *Bullseye Mail Sales*, 400 Hahn Road, Westminster, MD 21157.

Prices and numbers subject to change without notice. Valid in U.S. only.
All orders subject to availability. Please allow 4 to 6 weeks for delivery.

Need your books even faster? Call toll-free 1-800-793-2665
to order by phone and use your major credit card.
Please mention interest code 049-20 to expedite your order.